A Sick Obsession

By

Shawanda Carter

A Sick Obsession

Copyright © 2015 Shawanda Carter

Published by:

Write House Publishing under TIECE Presents

First Trade Paperback Edition Printing 2015

ISBN-13:9781517705510

ISBN-10:1517705517

Chapter 1

"Please, keep going. You know exactly how I like it," Darius informed the female that was taking pleasure in giving him some of the best head she could possibly give.

The female purred through pauses as if she was trying to catch her breath. "Ummmmmmmm," she cooed once more. Unbeknownst to her, she was not the only female for Darrius. In fact, she was one of many. This week, the female giving pleasure to Darrius was the new, young intern from Amina University. She had been shadowing him for a few months. Often his company would host a few interns from Amina University that were majoring in both Business and Architect, giving them real life experience. She was not really his type, but the fact that she did not mind giving him a much needed blowjob to help him start his workday was one of the main reasons he kept her around.

Darrius was to the point of his major release as he groaned, "AHHHH! Fuck, I'm about to bust... Shit...Shitttt..." Caught up in the moment he said, "Swallow it bitch! Yeah that's right, swallow it all up. Keep my shit clean," he added, pushing her head down further onto his long, thick penis. Just that quickly the fun was over and it was back to work for Darrius.

"How long are we going to keep this up, Darrius?" the intern asked.

"What do you mean by keep this up?" he questioned, fixing his pants as he walked back to his desk without even looking back at her. This was actually amusing to him, because it wasn't the first time that he'd been questioned with something of this nature.

"You know what I mean," she responded with an attitude.

Darrius was now getting a little irritated with the little tantrum that she was having rather quickly. It was all too common for him to have women act this way whenever he hooked up with what he called 'new pussy'. It had only been a few months and she was already attached to him. It was his own fault though, because she spent so much time with him. Usually when an intern came in they would shadow other people in the office, but the university felt it would be a great benefit if they were able to shadow an actual graduate that graduated from the university.

Darrius thought back to the first time when the new intern approached him in his office. She asked him if she could suck his dick. There was no shame in her game; she said she just wanted to taste him. Darrius grinned at the thought of how she looked when she saw how big his dick was. To his surprise, she was good at it. So, he had no problem letting her give him morning head service whenever time was available.

As good as her mouthpiece is, it's time to cut this needy bitch off, and the sooner the better, Darrius thought as he looked over at the anxious intern as she opened her mouth to talk.

"Why do you act as if we didn't just fuck like two animals in here?" she questioned like she was in denial of him rejecting her.

"First off, we did not fuck in here. You sucked my dick and swallowed my seeds," Darrius corrected her. "Secondly, you knew what you were getting yourself into when we first started doing this. So, don't act like you didn't know your role," he said bluntly, this time looking directly at her as he sat behind the desk in his office chair.

"You're a dick you know that Darrius?" she said.

"Yeah I know, and that's why you like it in your mouth all the time. Now if you would please excuse me, I have work to do," Darrius said as he looked down at his desk at the many things he had to get to before the day was over.

"Bitch," she whispered, rushing around the office and gathering her things as she quickly made her exit out of his office.

No more new pussy for me, Darrius thought to himself. Picking up his desk phone, he paged his secretary. Within a minute, she came through the door.

"Yes Mr. Jackson, do you need me?" she asked.

"Yes Martha," he quickly responded. "I need for you to make a call to whomever you need to at the University and please inform them that Jackson Corporations will no longer host interns."

"Why the sudden change in heart, Mr. Jackson?" Martha asked with a puzzled expression.

"It's just that, a change of heart. The last intern from Amina University did not work out as I thought she would."

Darrius explained.

"But Mr. Jackson, we have been in good standing with that school for so long," Martha countered.

"Martha!" Darrius said in a stern tone. "I did not call you in here for a debate. I called you in here to do as I asked," he said in a loud, aggressive tone.

"Yes sir," Martha said, almost dropping her head in defeat. "I do apologize," she added as she turned to exit his office.

"Oh, and by the way," Darrius said before she was completely out the door. "Have that new intern escorted off of the premises and inform her that she is no longer needed. She was getting too attached here," Darrius explained with a sly grin as he picked up the office phone on his desk.

Ring....Ring...Ring....

Why is she not picking up the phone? I know she sees me calling? Darrius thought. If I have to leave a voicemail there will be trouble when I get home. Just as he was thinking it, the answering machine picked up, asking him to leave a message. "Damn it!" he said as he slammed the phone down. "I will see her ass later."

As Darrius went about his workday, he glanced over to his desk clock and noticed that a few hours had passed and that his wife had still not called. Darrius walked out of his office to go check with his secretary to see if she may have called him back, hoping Martha may have forgotten to tell him. As he walked up to Martha's desk, he could see that she was talking with a woman. Once he was within view of the woman, her mouth seemed to have dropped as if she had just seen a celebrity. It didn't faze Darrius one bit being that he got this look all the time. In this case, he was not even concerned about it. He was more concerned about where his wife was and why she had not called him back.

Martha stood to her feet the minute she saw him coming. "Yes Mr. Jackson," she said. "If you called me I do apologize for not hearing you."

"No Martha, you're fine. I was just coming to see if my wife may have called." The wife comment did not seem to faze the staring woman, because she continued to stare and even lick her lips a little bit, as if she were saying, take me with her eyes. Usually this would amuse Darrius, but at this point, she was not a major factor as he looked past her. However, he did check the woman out rather quickly to the point that she may not have even noticed. From a quick glance he could tell that she was much older than he was, but yet she still was beautiful. Unfortunately, she wasn't his type though.

"No, Mrs. Jackson has not called," Martha answered, breaking him from his mental breakdown of the mystery woman. "Should I call her for you, Sir?" she asked.

"Yes, please do and once she is on the phone, please send the call to me, "Darrius stated as he turned to walk back towards his office.

Darrius seemed to have a major effect on women all his life, even at a young age. He grew up in a very loving and supportive family with strong family values. The Jackson family motto was family first and the extra shit last. At least that was what his father always told him and his brothers growing up. Darrius never had to struggle or want for anything. His father always provided for them and his mother took care of the home. Thinking back on his childhood, as he would so often do, he remembered how loving his parents were with one another. His mother never got upset with his father when he would be gone to work for long hours at a time. She would always welcome him with open arms and with a smile. Darrius valued that and promised himself that someday he too would have a marriage just like theirs. Therefore, once Darrius was of age and went off to college on a full scholarship to Amina University for both football and business, it was there that he first met Lizeth, his wife of eleven years now.

Lizeth was beautiful from the moment he laid eyes on her and he knew he had to have her. She stood out from the other women that he dealt with. She was about 5'7, and thick and curvy with a small waist. She had a body like Buffy, the video vixen. Darrius knew he would be with her. She had long, silky, black hair and the prettiest white teeth a person could have. She wore the best of clothes and always was well kept. Her booty was so big and juicy and Darrius, being an ass man, loved that.

Beyond all of her beauty, she was smart and fun which was what Darrius loved the most. She was studying law and even though he graduated before she did, they still dated and were married during her last year of school. She was the only woman, other than his mother, that had his heart. That has yet to change despite his occasional flings. No one would replace her. Just thinking about his wife was making him aroused and he wanted her now.

Darrius hit the intercom button on the phone that buzzed to his secretary. "Martha, has she called yet?" he asked.

"No sir, she has not," Martha answered. "I will keep you informed when she does, Sir," she added.

"Sure thing," Darrius said. He continued working for about an hour until he wasn't able to take it anymore. Darrius paged Martha and told her to hold his calls and to take messages, because he was leaving early for the day. He was heading home to find out why Lizeth was not answering her phone and to make sure she knew that he was pissed.

"Darrius has called me a million times and his secretary has left me an ass of messages," Lizeth said to Sam as they were walking to her car. Sam was a close friend of hers that she had known for a few years. They became close friends after working at a local Law Firm when Lizeth was just freshly coming out of her externship. Sam was the secretary there when she had started. They stopped hanging out once Lizeth left the firm after only being there for two years.

Recently, Sam had been begging her to hang out and take a yoga class with her. Finally, Lizeth agreed to try it.

"Now that was a great yoga class," Sam said, interrupting Lizeth as she was checking the many voicemail messages on her cell phone.

"Yeah, it was," Lizeth agreed, holding up her finger to quiet Sam so that she could hear her messages. Once they'd made it to the car, Lizeth paused to search for her car keys inside her gym bag. Lizeth then got inside of her car, as did

Sam. She started the engine to her 2015 Audi and then backed out of the parking lot of the gym.

"Girl don't trip. Darrius will be alright," Sam told her. "I do not think he would mind you going to yoga and keeping that body he so loves nice and fit," Sam said with a grin.

"Girl whatever," Lizeth said, rolling her eyes. "He probably freaked out because I am always available to him," she explained.

"Come on now, it can't be that serious," Sam snapped.

"It is," Lizeth said. She kept her eyes on the road, but she glanced over at her friend thinking, If only you knew.

"I don't get it, Lizeth. You act as if you're not supposed to leave the house. It's almost like you need damn permission. You're a grown ass woman," Sam told her, staring at the side of her face.

"You would not understand, Sam. Your ass is not married!" Lizeth shot back at her.

"So, because I'm not married I wouldn't understand?" Sam questioned.

"That's right," Lizeth replied.

"What's so funny is you're so blind it's pathetic. What you need to do is stop acting like a fucking trained lap dog," Sam said sarcastically.

"What is that supposed to mean, Sam?" Lizeth asked, anger in her voice. Sam did not respond. She just sat back and kept looking out the passenger side window with her arms folded across her chest.

"I am no one's lap dog, Sam. The next time you come at me like that your ass will be walking," she added and then pushed on the gas. She drove the rest of the way to her house in silence.

It had to be one of the longest, shortest rides that Lizeth had ever experienced. Upon pulling into the driveway, before she could even park good, it seemed that Sam was already out of the car. Apparently, the argument meant that they would not be speaking for a while since Sam headed straight to her car without saying another word.

I could care less, Lizeth thought. "How dare she come off on me like that? That chick got some real issues," Lizeth whispered to herself.

Sam got into her car and drove off quickly, not even giving Lizeth a second look.

Lizeth irritably rolled her eyes. She got some damn nerve, she thought, walking inside of her house to prepare dinner so that would be one less thing for Darrius to be pissed about.

Lizeth went into the kitchen and began cooking dinner. Once it was finished and the house was clean, she went upstairs to the large master bedroom to take a shower inside her gorgeous master bathroom. Lizeth loved her home, but her bathroom was her sanctuary. It had a large, cast concrete, garden sized tub and a wall of etched stone tiles that separated two distinct spa inspired shower areas. She could easily get lost in the bathroom as she glanced around the open space surrounding her. She also loved that the shower doors were made of glass so that she could easily see the entire bathroom while enjoying a shower or bath.

Darrius allowed Lizeth to decorate their immaculate home. He always said that it was part of a woman's work. Lizeth thought it was sweet of him, but then again a part of her felt a little insulted that he would consider it to be that way.

Lizeth undressed and stepped inside the shower. She allowed for the water to run down on her as it softly beat against her skin. She was thankful for the purifying system that Darrius had installed. The fresh water did them justice.

Lizeth was so into her shower that she did not even notice Darrius standing on the opposite side of the glass door staring at her. She turned the shower off and reached for a towel that was behind her on a shower rack inside the shower. She turned to walk out of the shower and came face to face with an angry Darrius looking at her.

Damn, she thought.

"Don't look so surprised," Darrius said.

"I wasn't expecting to see you so early," Lizeth said, sounding startled.

"Well, I wasn't expecting to have to leave work early either," Darrius responded. "What's wrong with your phone, Lizeth?" he asked.

"Nothing is wrong with it. I went to a yoga class with Sam today and I left it in the gym bag," she answered.

"Yoga? Since when were you into yoga?" Darrius asked.

"It was something new that I wanted to try and I enjoyed myself," Lizeth told him.

"Then why didn't you call me and let me know?" he angrily questioned.

"Call you? It was a split second thing that I decided to do," Lizeth answered, annoyed. "Why do I have to tell you my every move?"

"You're my wife, that's why," Darrius responded. "Sam is going to get your ass in trouble," he added. "Why all of a sudden do you want to go to a damn yoga class? What the hell do y'all have going on?" he asked.

"Darrius, why are you tripping? Sam has asked me to go with her before, but I kept turning her down," Lizeth said, becoming frustrated.

"Check your attitude, Lizeth," Darrius said sternly.

"What attitude?" she asked.

Darrius just looked at her."I will just have my dinner early and head back to the office," he said and walked out the bedroom.

"Are you serious?" Lizeth said.

Darrius did not respond. He just kept walking.

Later, Lizeth heard the vibrating sound of her cell phone going off. She walked over to her gym bag to retrieve it. It was a text message from Sam.

"Please do not be angry with me. I was out of line, I just enjoyed our time today. I never get to see you anymore and besides, we had fun."

Lizeth read over the text message again and smiled. Sam was right. They did have fun and it was nice to get out. Lizeth prided herself on making Darrius happy and being a good wife. Now it seemed that she'd forgotten about her own happiness. Lizeth had been thinking about going back to work, something that she definitely needed to discuss with Darrius. Lizeth recalled a time when she was working how it brought her joy. She was good at her job, but she gave it up to support Darrius.

I'm going back to work and I'm going to get out more. It's not like we have kids, Lizeth thought. Lizeth text messaged Sam back. "I will call you later to see what's next!" Lizeth

*****

"Back for the day, Mr. Jackson?" Martha asked as Darrius was getting off of the elevator walking towards his office.

"Yes, I'm back for the day. Do I have any messages?" Darrius asked.

"I've placed them on your desk. Oh, and you got a call from a Mr. Carter," Martha stated.

Darrius stopped and turned to face her. "As in Nelson Carter?" Darrius asked.

"Yes, how did you know? Were you expecting his call today?" Martha asked.

"No, I just heard he was in town and possibly looking to

do some work in this area," Darrius said with excitement in his voice. "Did he leave a message or a number?" Darrius asked.

"No sir, he did not. However, he was very persistent in meeting you in person. So, he is scheduled to come in tomorrow to see you at 3:30. I went ahead and put him on your schedule since your afternoon is free," Martha told him.

"Great job, Martha." Darrius said with enthusiasm. "He may be interested in possibly working with us."

"Possibly?" Martha questioned. "This could be great for the company."

"It could lead to even more projects," Darrius said.

"That would be great!" Martha said.

"Keep up the good work, Martha," Darrius told her.

"Yes sir," Martha replied. Martha was an excellent employee. She had worked for Darrius since he first opened the doors to his Architect Company. Darrius respected Martha to a certain degree, but he would never let her know that.

"Martha, I need you to get me all the information you can get on Mr. Carter and have it on my desk before you leave. That way I can be ready for tomorrow's meeting with him," Darrius ordered as he turned quickly to escape into his office.

As Darrius sat at his desk looking over the blueprint designs for a new club owner, he could not stop thinking about his meeting with Nelson Carter. Darrius knew who Nelson Carter was from word of mouth, but never met him. He was a successful businessman who owned several banks. Every year he would invest money into a few new projects where he would pay for affordable housing or fix up apartment communities in rural neighborhoods at little to no cost to the tenants.

Nelson Carter had a lot of love for humanity and helping people of all kinds. Nelson Carter's name alone carried a lot of weight. He got respect because of all the great work he did. Anything that involved giving back he was attached to it. Working with Nelson would be a great opportunity for any company.

What an amazing prospect this would be to have, Darrius thought to himself. Filled with excitement, he put the blueprints aside to read up on Mr. Carter and to get an idea of what his next project would be. Not only could this bring in more money, but more business as well. It wasn't that he was hurting for it. However, he was determined to get the deal and push everything else aside.

Chapter 2

"So you were serious about going back to work?" Sam screamed into the phone.

"I told you I was," Lizeth said, holding the phone as she drunk her morning coffee.

"Girl I am happy for you. It's time you got out of that damn house. So, what does Darrius has to say about it?" Sam asked.

"I tried to wait up for him last night, but he came home too damn late," Lizeth answered.

"Oh," Sam said.

"I tried talking to him this morning but he was in a rush so I sent him a text explaining what I wanted to do," Lizeth said.

"Damn girl, you're serious," Sam giggled.

"Whatever girl, I am just so ready to get back to work," Lizeth sighed.

"Well hopefully he will understand," Sam said.

"Yeah I hope so too. I have been out of work for almost two years."

"Damn it's been that long?" Sam said.

"Yes too damn long," Lizeth said.

"Well I am on my way to your house," Sam told her.

"Okay, see you soon," Lizeth said and hung up the phone. I love the way I'm feeling,' Lizeth thought and smiled to herself.

*****

"What is this long ass text from Lizeth?" Darrius said, looking down at his phone as he sat in the parking lot at his job.

"Darrius I have been doing a lot of thinking and I think it's time I went back to work. I understand that I said that I would stop working and become a stay at home wife because you said you didn't want me working, however that is not what I want anymore. I have been out of work for too long

19

and I really want to get back into it. I supported you when you started up your company and all I ask is you support me with my decision to go back into the work force.".

Darrius stopped reading the text as he was becoming angry. Has she lost her damn mind? She's still going on with this bullshit? Darrius thought. Darrius yelled in his car as he punched the wheel. Not today, I do not need this today, he thought to himself. I will have to deal with her later.

Darrius took a deep breath, closed his eyes, and just sat in silence for a few minutes. I have to be on point today, Darrius thought. Darrius then shot a quick text back to Lizeth. "The answer is no, we will talk later." He got out his car and headed into his office to prepare for his meeting with Mr. Carter.

*****

"I cannot believe he told me no. I am not some damn child!" Lizeth said to Sam as they were leaving the gym.

"He got some damn nerve, he wouldn't be telling me no," Sam said.

"Yeah you right, I didn't go to law school to let it go to waste," Lizeth said.

"I know that's right girl," Sam agreed.

"He needs to stop trying to make me be like his mother," Lizeth said.

Sam gave her a confusing look. "Wait, what? What do you mean like his mother?" Sam asked, grabbing Lizeth by the arm.

"Well when Darrius was growing up his father was the breadwinner in the house and his mother was the housewife. Darrius has always wanted that," Lizeth explained.

"That explains why he doesn't want you working," Sam said.

"But now it's not what I want. In the beginning it was okay and I didn't mind, but I was hoping that it didn't have to be forever. I would like to get back to work. I was just starting to make a name for myself," Lizeth said.

"Well if it means that much to you, then you should go back to it no matter what," Sam advised.

"After our little confrontation it did get me to thinking that I have changed. I do not want to be a housewife," Lizeth said.

"Just like me to cause trouble," Sam said with a grin.

"No you didn't. It just made me realize how I've been asleep for too long. I'm wide awake now," Lizeth said.

"I agree with you, do what makes you happy," Sam said.

"I want to be able to move without him knowing my every move. I am sure there are things he does that he does not tell me," Lizeth said.

"You think so?" Sam asked.

"Hell yeah," Lizeth said.

"So now that you're sure on what you're going to do, let's head out to grab some food," Sam said, quickly changing the subject.

"Yeah, I am hungry and clear on my choice," Lizeth said. Change is in the air, Lizeth thought as they got into her car. "In fact, I think I will be going to Darrius' job to see him," Lizeth announced.

"Sounds like trouble," Sam said. Lizeth just looked at her and gave her a big smile.

****

"Come on, you know I have to head back to work," Darrius said.

"Please stay a little longer, I only get to see you so often," the female voice said.

"No, I have a lot of work to take care of and I cannot be

late. You know how it is," Darrius said as he put back on his clothes.

"Fine, then when will I see you again?" she pouted.

"I will let you know when I need you," Darrius replied while he grabbed his suit jacket and left the woman's condominium without looking back. Darrius was beginning to think he was getting sloppy with his outside marital adventures. Martha left a message saying that his wife called the office six times today. She must be calling because I said no to her wanting to go back to work. I don't mind her going out to yoga, but work? Darrius thought. Work was not an option and the answer is still no.

After going home to shower up and put on something sexy, Lizeth thought, what would be better than to drop by her husband's office? She called six times and the secretary told her that Mr. Jackson was out. That was somewhat weird. He did mention he had a meeting today so why is he not at work? That was the first crazy thing that happened today. The other was when Lizeth walked into the office to ask to speak with her husband, only to be looked at as if she was a lying about who she was. "Martha I take it?" Lizeth asked as she approached the desk.

"Yes that is my name, may I help you?" Martha asked.

Martha was a middle-aged woman with blonde-hair. She dressed very nicely and neat. You could tell she may have had some work done. Her face looked of someone who just got injected with Botox. Her nails were fresh and her jewelry was beautiful. Darrius never spoke a lot about her, but whenever she called the office it was Martha she had to talk to.

"Yes I would like to see my husband," Lizeth said.

"Excuse me if I look surprised, but who is your husband and are you sure he works here?" Martha asked. That took Lizeth by surprise.

I can understand her not knowing me from the fact that I have never been to the office, but I am sure Darrius has at least have a picture or shown one to his employees. "Yes, my husband works here," Lizeth said, a little annoyed and shocked. "In fact, my husband is your boss, and I will wait in his office for him," Lizeth said as she stormed past her desk and went towards Darrius' office. Where is he? she wondered.

"Excuse me. Excuse me but you can't just walk into Mr. Jackson's office and claim to be his wife," Martha said, rushing behind her. "I have talked to his wife and it is not you," Martha added.

24

Lizeth turned around to face Martha. "I assure you that he is my husband and you have spoken to me," Lizeth said. Lizeth glanced around the office to see if she could see any pictures and noticed none.

"I do apologize but you cannot wait in here, Mr. Jackson has many people who come to see him," Martha said.

"Well I am his wife," Lizeth said.

"Well why haven't I seen you before? You can be anyone," Martha said.

"What did you just say?" Lizeth asked.

*****

What is the commotion going on in my office? Darrius wondered as he exited the elevator. Once he reached his office, he could see Martha and some woman dressed in some very appealing clothing having what looked like an argument.

"What did you mean by that?"he heard the woman ask.

"Please, I need you to leave," Martha said.

"What is the problem here?" Darrius interrupted. Both ladies turned to face him.

"Mr. Jackson, I do apologize, but again you have an

25

unannounced visitor," Martha said, walking over to him.

"So I am unannounced Darrius?" Lizeth said.

"Lizeth," Darrius said. "Martha, I would like you to meet my wife," Darrius said.

With shock in her eyes, Martha looked apologetically at Lizeth and said sorry without saying a word, it was all in her eyes.

"It's okay, you were only doing your job," Lizeth said.

"Martha, could you please leave my office and close the door? I need to speak to my wife," Darrius said, staring at Lizeth.

"Yes sir," Martha said as she rushed out the office. I will deal with her later, Darrius thought.

"So is something wrong?" Darrius asked.

"Do I need a reason to come see you Darrius?" Lizeth asked, looking confused.

"Yes you do. I have a secretary and if you can't reach me you go through her," Darrius said.

"I wanted to surprise you," Lizeth said.

"Well I am surprised, but now is not a good time. I have a major meeting," Darrius said, walking over to his office chairs and sitting.

"You clearly don't look happy at all to see me."

"What are you talking about?" Darrius asked.

"If you have such a big meeting then where were you?" Lizeth asked. The fact that she was questioning him caught him off guard.

He was just in a meeting with one of his side women, but he knew he could not tell her that so he had to think of something.

"I took a late lunch," Darrius lied.

"It's 2:15 you always take lunch at 11:00," Lizeth said, looking confused.

"Well I felt like taking a late lunch," Darrius said.

"This wouldn't have anything to do with me wanting to go back to work would it?" Lizeth asked, throwing her hands in the air.

"What? You still on that?" Darrius asked. "I made up my mind on that, it is not up for discussion!" Darrius yelled.

"Like hell," Lizeth muttered as she turned to head for the door.

Darrius jumped up from the chair, rushed Lizeth and grabbed her around her waist.Darrius had to admit his wife looked even more beautiful when she was upset, but he had to take control of the situation and quickly.

"Let me go Darrius," Lizeth said as she tried to get

away.

"Lizeth I don't know what's gotten into you lately, but it will stop," Darrius said as he turned her to face him. Darrius started walking backward until they were up against the exterior wall in his office, furthest away from the door. "Then you come into my office looking sexy, oh I know what you really came here for," Darrius said with hunger in his eyes.

Lizeth stared at her husband. Despite being mad, she knew what he was doing and no matter how much she wanted to be upset she knew she could not resist him.

"Beg for it," Darrius said, staring in his wife eyes and licking his lips.

Those lips, I want to feel them on my body, she thought to herself. "I want you Darrius," Lizeth said, staring at his lips.

"I know," Darrius smirked. He placed his hands underneath her dress and ripped off her panties, forcefully kissing her. He then placed his hands onto her upper thighs and pulled them apart. He lifted her up with one hand and placed the other around her neck. He turned her around so that her back was up against the wall. He took his hand, found her hotspot and placed two fingers inside of her. She was already wet with excitement.

Lizeth threw her head back and closed her eyes, moaning so sweetly. Darrius moved his fingers deep inside of her, in and out, causing Lizeth to lose control. She had already cum on his fingers and he had not even fucked her yet.

Darrius could not hold out any longer. Her moans were making his dick hard, he could feel it through his pants. He unzipped his pants and allowed them and his boxers to hit the floor. He then removed his soaked fingers and placed them in her mouth, making her taste her own juices, which she did willingly. He put his massive dick in her while she sucked his fingers as if they gave her life. He began to pound into her like he had never before.

"Shiit... babe," Darrius moaned.

"Yes...fuck me Darr...ius," Lizeth said, as if trying to catch her next wind.

"Yeah, you want this don't you?" Darrius asked as he stroked her deeper and deeper. Her moans got louder and louder.

She came here for this, Darrius thought while he ripped inside of her. That thought alone made him stroke harder. He could feel her cumming on his dick, but he was not there yet.

He was mad and horny all at the same time, so many emotions. Harder and harder he stroked. "Ahh, Ahh! Damn baby," Darrius moaned.

Lizeth couldn't handle it any longer, she was about to explode again. He was fucking her like an animal and if he didn't stop, she wouldn't be able to walk out of there. Darrius had a grip on her and he was not about to let her go.

Darrius was so caught up in the hot sex he was having that he completely forgot about his meeting. Had it not been for Martha buzzing him that Mr. Carter was on the phone they would have been still going at it. Darrius knew that was important, but the timing couldn't have been worse. Damn and I haven't got my nut yet, he thought, pounding harder and deeper to get the satisfaction he was aiming for. Darrius looked into Lizeth eyes and gave her a long passionate kiss. "I've got business to get to," Darrius said, breathing hard.

"I know," Lizeth smiled.

Darrius let Lizeth down and rushed into his office bathroom to freshen up. When he came back out Lizeth had already left. "Damn I guess she got what she needed," Darrius chuckled and walked over to his desk to answer the phone.

Darrius took a deep breath before picking up the phone.

"Good Afternoon Mr. Carter, this is Darrius Jackson," he said into the phone.

"Good afternoon Mr. Jackson. It's a pleasure to finally talk with you today, and please call me Nelson," the man's voice on the other end said.

"Sure," Darrius said with a smile.

"Well as you know Mr. Jackson, I scheduled to come in to meet with you today, but unfortunately I am not able to do so since something else came up," Nelson informed him.

"Well that's okay. Things do come up, would you like to reschedule for another time?" Darrius asked.

"Well I was hoping that I could still meet with you today," Nelson said.

"Oh okay, my office hours are from eight to five. Would you like to just try tomorrow?" Darrius asked.

"Maybe I need to be clearer. I would like to meet with you outside of your office. Maybe come to your home," Nelson said.

"That would be fine," Darrius agreed.

"Great! What would be a good time for you?" Nelson asked.

"How does 8:30 sound?" Darrius said.

"Sounds good Mr. Jackson, I will see you at 8:30

tonight," Nelson said and hung up the phone. Darrius put the phone back on the receiver, excited and happy for the chance to possibly do business with someone who could bring in more business for his company. At that moment Darrius realized that he didn't give Nelson his address.

"Martha," Darrius called out.

*****

That man, that man! Lizeth thought to herself as she sat in her car in front of her house. The thought of what just happened to her in her husband's office brought a smile to her face. Her phone buzzed, letting her know she had a text message. It was a text from Darrius. "Oh he wants round two," Lizeth said, opening the text.

"Hey, babe I really enjoyed that afternoon special with you. Lol but I have a potential client coming over for dinner around 8: 30 so make dinner extra special tonight. Thanks!"

He has some damn nerve, Lizeth thought to herself as she got out of her car. Lizeth walked inside of her house and went upstairs. "Dinner will have to wait," Lizeth muttered as she started a hot bath for herself. Her body was sore after that run in with Darrius, her body needed this soak.

Lizeth finally got out of the hot tub and headed downstairs to prepare a dinner. Now what am I going to cook with such short notice ?she wondered as she glanced in her refrigerator. I know what I can do! I will invite Sam over because I cannot deal with this on my own, Lizeth thought as she picked up her phone and called Sam. Sam did not answer so she left a voicemail and then sent her a text. Moments later Sam text back saying she would be over shortly. At least with Sam there she wouldn't have to do this dinner alone. Lizeth went into the kitchen to see what she had. She looked for something simple since she didn't have much notice or time to prepare. She decided on some boneless chicken with asparagus and mashed potatoes.

Ding, Dong!

That must be Sam, she got here rather quickly, Lizeth thought as she was putting her chicken into the oven. "I am coming," Lizeth yelled. Lizeth ran to the front door to find Sam standing there with a bottle of wine in her hand.

"Hey girl," Sam greeted her, entering the house.

"Hey," Lizeth said back, giving her a hug.

"I am so happy you came," Lizeth said.

"Girl I know how you feel when you get hit with something at the last minute," Sam laughed.

"I know right, no notice!" Lizeth said as they walked toward the kitchen.

"So who is the person coming over?" Sam asked.

"I am not sure, he didn't say," Lizeth answered.

"Oh okay," Sam shrugged.

"Anyway, I had an eventful day," Lizeth said as she placed the wine into the fridge to get cool.

"You did?" Sam said.

"Yes! I decided to surprise Darrius at work today," Lizeth told her.

"Really, how did that go?" Sam asked.

"Well before I went up there I called and the secretary told me he was not there. I didn't want to go up there and he not be there, so I called back six times," Lizeth said.

"So where was he?" Sam asked slyly.

"He said he took his lunch late," Lizeth said. "Then I just went up there because I got tired of calling."

"Okay, so what happened when you got there?" Sam asked.

"Well for one, the secretary didn't have a clue as to who I was," Lizeth said.

"How is that possible?" Sam asked.

"Well I never really went up there before," Lizeth said.

"That's weird. It's your husband's company. How did you manage that?"Sam asked.

"I don't know," Lizeth sighed.

"Some support you are!" Sam said, rolling her eyes.

"What?" Lizeth asked, in defensive mode.

"Oh I am just joking girl," Sam laughed.

"Well I never had a reason to, but back to what I was saying," Lizeth said, trying to finish her story. "It was a mess and we got into it for a few minutes because she wouldn't let me in his office," Lizeth said.

"Can you blame her?" Sam asked.

"Bitch, whose side are you on?" Lizeth scolded. Sam shook her head and smiled.

"Anyway," Lizeth continued. "Darrius got there and he and I got into it, then we really got into it in his office if you know what I mean," Lizeth smiled.

"No, what do you mean?" Sam asked.

Lizeth gave Sam a puzzled look and shook her head. "Well I will put it so you can understand. He fucked me good in his office!" Lizeth grinned.

"You so nasty!" Sam said.

"He loves it," Lizeth shrugged.

"Girl, can you pour me a glass of wine or something?

This conversation is getting a little too nasty for me," Sam said.

"Since when was that an issue?"Lizeth said as she walked over to the fridge to retrieve some wine she had previously opened.

Sam grabbed two glasses from the cabinet. "Was Darrius upset when you showed up?" Sam asked.

"Yes, but for only a second," Lizeth said.

"Maybe you shouldn't pop up on him like that, he might not like surprises," Sam advised.

"Are you okay? That's my husband, he loves surprises," Lizeth said.

"Well you just said he was upset," Sam reminded her.

"Yes for a second, but he got over it once he got in between these legs," Lizeth said amusingly.

"Could you please stop talking about having sex with Darrius?" Sam snapped.

Lizeth looked at Sam and her face was unreadable. "What's wrong with you?" Lizeth asked.

"Nothing, I just don't think it's necessary for you to talk about your sex life with Darrius," Sam said.

"What? You can't be serious!" Lizeth said.

"I am! How do you think he would feel if he knew you

did that?" Sam said.

"Wait, since when did you care about how Darrius felt?" Lizeth asked.

"I don't, I'm just saying," Sam said.

"Yeah I bet. But let me be concerned for my husband, not you," Lizeth said.

"Fine," Sam said.

"You are acting strange," Lizeth said.

"No, it's just that I don't want to hear about you and your husband's sex life," Sam said wryly.

"Well I understand that, but I was starting to think you had a thing for my husband," Lizeth said jokingly. Sam nearly spit her wine out her mouth.

"That is crazy," Sam said nervously as she cleaned her mouth.

"I was just kidding girl," Lizeth said.

"Well I did not find that funny," Sam said with an attitude.

"Please, you may need to stop drinking that wine, you extra sensitive tonight," Lizeth said.

Sam rolled her eyes at her. "Whatever," Sam mumbled, looking down at her phone.

"Are you expecting a call?" Lizeth asked as she noticed

Sam checking her phone yet again.

"Uhmm, no... What are you talking about?" Sam replied.

"I've noticed that you have checked your phone a few times since you walked in the door," Lizeth said.

"No I haven't, I am just looking at the time," Sam said.

"Oh is that what it is? If you have somewhere to be, then go," Lizeth said.

"If I have somewhere to be, why are you jumping down my throat?" Sam asked.

"I am not jumping down your throat. All I said is if you have somewhere to be then go ahead!" Lizeth yelled.

Sam closed her eyes and took a deep breath. "Please don't yell at me again," Sam said calmly.

Lizeth rolled her eyes and threw her hands up. "Yeah whatever," Lizeth said as she went to the stove to turn off her food. "I don't know what your issue is but you need to chill," Lizeth said as she turned around to see Sam standing right behind her, which startled her.

"I don't have an issue, maybe you do," Sam said with a blank stare. Lizeth backed up into the stove to get a little space between her and Sam. She was so close that Lizeth could hear her breathing. Her hands started shaking. "What is my issue?" Lizeth asked, staring into Sam's face.

Sam did not say anything she just had an absent look on her face. "Oh never mind, I was just playing," Sam said as she backed up. "Just for future reference I don't care to hear about you having sex with your husband," Sam said.

"You make it seem like I went into details!" Lizeth said.

"Still, some things are to be shared between a husband and wife only," Sam said.

"I guess," Lizeth shrugged. Sam's phone started to vibrate uncontrollably. "Are you going to answer that?" Lizeth asked her, gesturing to her cell phone.

"Oh yeah, I will call them back. So when does Darrius get off?" Sam asked.

"Five," Lizeth answered.

"Oh," Sam said.

"What time do you have?" Lizeth asked.

"I got 5:15," Sam answered.

"Oh he should be pulling up in few minutes," Lizeth said. Sam's phone started to vibrate even more.

"Well it looks like I won't be able to stay after all. I got something I need to do," Sam said.

"Oh okay, it sounds important," Lizeth said.

"It is, I will call you later," Sam said as she rushed out the kitchen.

39

I can't say I am mad to see her go, Lizeth thought, thinking on how close she was standing behind her. Oh well, let me get my dinner out the oven. As she placed the food on the counter she noticed her large butcher knife on the counter that wasn't there before. Where did that come from? she wondered. She shrugged it off and proceeded to prepare dinner.

Chapter 3

Darrius walked into the house to get ready for his dinner with Nelson. When he walked into the kitchen he found Lizeth sitting there with a glass of wine, staring straight ahead. She looked as if she were puzzled about something. Darrius walked over to her, placed his hands around her waist and kissed her on her neck.

"Hey baby," he greeted her.

"Hey," Lizeth said.

"Is something wrong?" Darrius asked.

"I have to get ready," Lizeth said as she walked out of the kitchen and went upstairs to get dressed. Darrius followed her upstairs to their bedroom.

"What's wrong?" Darrius asked again.

Lizeth shrugged her shoulders, shook her head as if to say nothing and walked inside of her massive walk-in closet.

Darrius' shoulder started to tighten up, even the air in the room felt thick. Something is up, Darrius thought, but he knew he did not want to get into it with Lizeth before dinner with Nelson. However, he knew he had to say something or whatever it was would only get worse.

"Did I do something?" Darrius asked.

Lizeth walked out of her closet. "No," she responded.

"Well what's wrong?" Darrius asked.

"Nothing, we can talk about it later," Lizeth said as she went back into the closet.

"Ok, well I am about to go take a quick shower and get ready," Darrius said, walking toward the bathroom.

Lizeth got dressed and went back downstairs to finish preparing dinner. She was starting to feel the wine she had been drinking. Lizeth put on some soft music while she prepared everything. She was so into what she was doing that she did not hear Darrius walk into the dining room talking to her. "Lizeth did you hear me?" Darrius asked.

"What did you say? I didn't see you there," Lizeth said.

"I said everything looks nice," Darrius assured.

"Oh thank you, I do try," Lizeth smiled.

"Well I will be back. I'm about to go to the wine cellar and get a nice bottle of wine," Darrius said as he turned and walked out of the kitchen.

"All right, you might need to bring up more than one," Lizeth called after him.

It was about 8:25 when the door bell rung. Lizeth was just finishing placing all the dinnerware onto the table. Darrius was still in the wine cellar getting some wine to drink. She went to answer the door and once she opened it she found a very attractive man standing there. He had a light complexion, dark hair and a build that was similar to Darrius, very athletic.

"I take it that you're Mr. Carter?" Lizeth greeted him, opening the door wider to let him in.

"Yes I am, and please call me Nelson," Nelson smiled.

"Sure thing," she replied as she motioned for him to come in.

"Well you have a lovely home," Nelson complimented as he entered, looking around.

"Thank you," Lizeth said. "Would you like me to take your coat and maybe get you something to drink?" Lizeth asked.

"That would be fine Mrs. Jackson."

"You can call me Lizeth, you don't have to be so formal," Lizeth said with a laugh. "I will take your coat and get you that drink, as well as find my husband," Lizeth said.

"Thank you," Nelson said.

Darrius retrieved the bottles of wine from his cellar, which was a collection of the best of the best as far as wine went. He took the bottles into the kitchen to Lizeth and she informed him that Nelson was in the living room. He walked into the living room to greet Nelson who was standing near his window looking out.

"Good Afternoon Nelson," Darrius said. Nelson turned around and extended his hand to Darrius.

"Good Afternoon Mr. Jackson, it is a pleasure to finally meet you," Nelson said.

"Likewise, please call me Darrius," Darrius said as he shook his hand."Please have a seat, "he offered, gesturing to the sofa.

"So Darrius, you have a lovely home and a beautiful wife, tell me how a man like you keeps it all together?" Nelson asked.

"Well, I do value hard work in whatever it is that I do, whether it's work or marriage," Darrius said.

"That's a good way to be, and that's exactly why I

wanted the chance to meet with you," Nelson said. "I find that a man who has honor, respect for family and a strong work ethic is a great plus and that's the kind of person I would like to work with," Nelson said.

"I agree with you on that and thanks for the compliment," Darrius said.

Lizeth walked in carrying a tray with drinks on it. "Here are those drinks for you gentlemen," Lizeth said. "Dinner should be ready in a few more minutes," she added.

Both men smiled as she placed the tray down and left the room. Darrius noticed how calm Lizeth was. Maybe she has had too much to drink. I just hope she can keep it together tonight, he thought.

"Tell me how you two met. Were you in college?" Nelson asked.

"Well yes, that's exactly where we met," Darrius replied. "That was a good guess," Darrius stated.

"Well Darrius, I like to know who I may be dealing with so I do a little research. I am sure that you did the same on me," Nelson said, drinking his wine and staring over the rim of the glass at him. Darrius was unsure of what to feel about that or if it was becoming something weird.

"Yes, you're right, I did do my research on you. Only

routine things, like wanting to know what it is your working on, but never worrying about your personal life," Darrius emphasized.

"So what did you find out about me Darrius?" Nelson asked as he placed his drink down.

"Well for starters, you love to give back to the community, most of your projects are to help areas that could use support and you have banks that are located all over the world," Darrius answered.

"Correct, and I am a strong believer in giving back. I hope I am not making you feel uncomfortable, I just like to know who a person really is," Nelson explained.

"I understand that, but what does a person's personal life have to do with how they handle business?" Darrius asked.

"Most people's character is really seen when they are not at their nine to five," Nelson rationalized."See, what you read about me is all me, there are no secrets with me. It is all out there," Nelson said.

"Well I think any person is entitled to some form of privacy," Darrius said.

"I agree with that as well, but what needs to be private if you have nothing to hide?" Nelson declared. "I do background checks on everyone I plan to do business with beforehand, that way I can really know who they are versus what they want people to know," Nelson said.

If he is saying what I think he is then he knows a lot more about me than he is putting on, Darrius thought.

Nelson looked at Darrius in a serious manner. "You seem nervous Darrius."

"Why would I be nervous?" Darrius asked.

"I notice that your hands are shaking and you spilled wine onto your carpet," Nelson said, pointing to the floor.

"So what is that all about?" Lizeth said as she stood in the hallway, looking at Nelson and Darrius as they sat staring at each other until Nelson pointed to some wine on the carpet. They didn't even notice that she was standing there listening to them. She was about to walk in to tell them that dinner was ready, but she stopped when she overheard Nelson say that Darrius seemed nervous. What is going on in here? she wondered. As long as she knew her husband there has never been anyone to make him nervous enough to spill expensive wine, but from where she was standing she could tell that Nelson did.

"Dinner is ready," Lizeth announced, entering into the living room. Both men stood up and walked into the dining area to a well-prepared spread. They all sat down and blessed the food and the mood went from tense to comfortable. Whatever it was that happened in the living room was long gone.

"Nelson, do you have family around here?" Lizeth asked, not realizing that she was rather loud.

"Sweetheart, I think you have had a little too much to drink," Darrius said with a smile.

"You may be right, I do apologize," Lizeth said as she moved her half-filled glass of wine away from her.

"I think it's fine, it's good to get loose sometimes, Nelson said, smiling at Lizeth. "To answer your question, I do have family around here but most of my family is in New York," Nelson answered.

"Okay. Is your family big?" Lizeth asked.

"It's rather big," Nelson said.

"I don't think Nelson wants to be asked about his family Lizeth," Darrius interrupted.

"It's okay with me Darrius. Besides, your wife is too beautiful to just sit here and be quiet," Nelson said, staring at him as if he can see through him.

What is up with this guy? Darrius wondered.

"I hope I am not being disrespectful, but I am sure you realize how beautiful your wife is," Nelson said. Darrius

48

nodded in agreement."Lizeth, tell me about yourself, what kind of work do you do now? I read somewhere that you were one your way to being a damn good lawyer then all of a sudden you left it all behind," Nelson said.

"She is a wife now," Darrius interrupted. Nelson and Lizeth looked over to Darrius who was staring at Nelson with irritation.

"Well Darrius, I was not trying to offend you in anyway, but I believe she can answer for herself," Nelson said.

"No offense taken, but I already answered your question, therefore she has answered," Darrius said firmly.

"You are correct, I can speak for myself," Lizeth said as she gave Darrius a sarcastic look. "Well I grew up around here in Tennessee. I had both my parents in the home and they both worked. My father was a Lawyer and my mother was a Registered Nurse until both retired. I am an only child," Lizeth responded.

"Wow that is great. So you followed behind your father practicing law?" Nelson asked.

"Yes I did. He was the reason I was able to find employment so quickly," Lizeth admitted.

"It's not often you find women who follow their fathers in careers. I find that amazing," Nelson said.

"Well I've always like law as long as I could remember," Lizeth said.

"Well I think you should get back into it, they could use you out there," Nelson implied. Lizeth glanced over to Darrius, unsure of what to say.

"Well how about some dessert?" Darrius said, changing the subject.

"Sure. I will go and get that," Lizeth said, getting up from the table.

"Nelson I don't mind you having dinner in my home, but I would appreciate it if you stop trying to boost my wife's head up about a career she once had that she decided to give up," Darrius said.

"You mean stop telling her the truth," Nelson stated.

"What?" Darrius asked.

"Your wife was great at her job and she could have been greater. Did you not see how her eyes light up when I mentioned it?" Nelson asked.

"You're out of line Nelson and I would like it if all questions from here on out be about business and business only," Darrius said.

"Sure, if that's what you want Mr. Jackson then that's what it will be," Nelson said. "One thing though," Nelson said.

"What is that?" Darrius asked.

"Did your wife give up her career because she wanted to or because she did it for you?"

Once Lizeth came back into the dining room, she again found the two men staring at each other. It seemed that every time she left she walked back into something else.

"Okay, I have some cherry pie and ice cream," Lizeth offered. "I hope that is okay with everyone," she added.

"That sounds good," Nelson nodded.

"Great," Lizeth smiled as she served the men their pie.

"Well I will leave you two to talk as I have a kitchen to clean," Lizeth said.

"It was nice meeting you Mrs. Jackson and the meal was wonderful," Nelson complimented, getting up from his chair to shake her hand. "I look forward to hopefully seeing you again," he added.

"You may call me Lizeth and thank you, it was a pleasure to meet you as well," Lizeth said as she went back into the kitchen.

"Well I do hope this evening was not that bad," Nelson said, sitting back down to enjoy his pie.

"No it was not that bad," Darrius said, looking at him

"We just have to understand the boundaries and we will be just fine."

"What are your boundaries Mr. Jackson?" Nelson asked.

"Simple. My personal life is off limits. I don't want you asking about my personal life and I will do the same. It's just business at all times, if that is still on the table," Darrius responded.

"The opportunity is still there Mr. Jackson," Nelson said.

"That's good to know," Darrius said.

"If that's how you want it, then it will be just business with us two," Nelson agreed. "Well I seem to be getting a little full and I think it's time for me to leave," Nelson said.

"I will walk you to the door," Darrius said. As they walked towards the front door, Darrius called out to Lizeth to bring Mr. Carter's coat.

"Again, it was a pleasure to meet you both. Hope you both enjoy the rest of your evening," Nelson said as he went out the door.

"I will walk you out," Darrius said as he escorted Nelson to his car.

"I do hope that this evening did not damage our chances of working together," Darrius said as they walked to Nelson's awaiting limo.

"Well I don't think it did much damage Mr. Jackson. You're a man who wants everyone to know the rules beforehand," Nelson said. "Just as I," he added.

"Thank you for understanding that," Darrius said.

"No problem," Nelson replied as his driver got out of the limo to open the door for him. "Besides Mr. Jackson, I will be seeing you again. I will call to set something up with your secretary. If that is ok with you," Nelson said, getting inside of the limo.

"That would be fine," Darrius said with a sigh of relief. Maybe we can salvage this after all.

"Good night Mr. Carter." Nelson rolled down the window of the limo and waved. As Darrius turned around to walk towards the house, Nelson's limo stopped and he motioned for Darrius to come back to the back window. "Just one thing Mr. Jackson. I want you to understand that since we are strictly business that you are my business now and I know everything about you," Nelson informed him.

"So what are you saying?"Darrius asked.

"Well at this point, you could have the chance to work alongside me. However, there is the matter of your personal affairs. I will need you to be fully committed," Nelson said.

"I don't have any personal affairs that would hinder this

potential partnership," Darrius said.

"Don't patronize me. The first thing with me is you have to remain honest and truthful. If not, then how can I trust you?" Nelson said.

"You're right, but I assure you that I don't have anything that would cause any kind of friction," Darrius insisted.

Nelson just looked at Darrius and for a minute, he said nothing. He finally spoke. "Mr. Jackson, your personal affairs that I am referring to will not just hurt you. I am speaking on the several women you have outside of your marriage," Nelson stated.

Darrius was stunned. He knew that this is what he was hinting at earlier but he knew that he had been careful. He wondered how he found out. I can't believe this shit, Darrius thought. He was at a loss for words. His secret was out and now he had to see what it was that Nelson Carter wanted to do with it.

"I will contact you Darrius," Nelson said as he rolled up the window and drove off, leaving Darrius there standing at a loss for words.

Why is he just standing there? Lizeth wondered as she watched her husband and Mr. Nelson talk. I don't know what it is with those two but it's strange. One minute they are relaxed and calling each other by first name, and next they are formal, calling each other by last name. What a roller coaster! she thought, shaking her head.

Lizeth open the door to call Darrius inside but he was coming in as she was opening the door. "Why were you standing their looking lost?"she asked.

"No reason," Darrius said, walking past her.

"Darrius what is wrong with you? You entire mood has changed," Lizeth called to him as he walked past her and went up the stairs.

"No it hasn't, you just in your feelings." Darrius yelled back. Lizeth was furious and went after him.

"How am I in my feelings?" Lizeth asked, coming in the room behind him. Darrius went and sat on the bed to remove his clothing.

"I don't feel like talking about this, I have to get some rest," Darrius said.

"Fine. Just so you know, I will be calling the firm I use to work for to see if they have a place for me. If they do I will be going back to work," Lizeth said. Darrius got up from the bed and walked towards Lizeth.

"What part of I don't want you working did you not get?" Darrius said, staring at her with a tight jaw.

"Darrius I am a grown woman and I only stopped working because of you, but now I want to go back to work," Lizeth said.

"Why can't you just understand that I am the man? I work and you stay home!" Darrius said.

"I am not okay with that any more Darrius. I stopped for a while until you got your business up and running and now that you do, I think it's a good time to rejoin the work force," she told him defiantly.

"I don't give a damn if you are or not! I said no. Everybody keeps putting these ideas in your head that you need to go back to work when you really don't!" Darrius yelled.

"You're not open to compromise at all are you?" Lizeth asked.

"What compromise? I just said what was going to happen, so miss me with all that other shit you talking," Darrius snapped. "Look, I am about to head out for a minute, I just need to clear my head," Darrius said.

"Where are you going Darrius?"

"If I wanted you to know I would tell you," Darrius said over his shoulder as he walked out the room.

Darrius had been riding around for a while after leaving

the house, contemplating on what had just happened. That was an odd meeting with Nelson. A man I've only known for a short moment knows more about me than just business. What's his angle? I think he may have had me followed, or someone is talking to him. I guess he really does mean it when he says he has to know who he is getting in business with.

He tried to think of who could have talked but he kept coming up blank. No one really knew about his personal affairs like that anyway. "I wonder what it is he wants then?" Darrius said aloud. Then Lizeth wants to go back to work, even after we agreed that she would become a homemaker. I need a drink. Hmmm, I know something that would be better than a drink. Darrius pulled out his phone and dialed a number and a woman answered the phone. "Hi sweetheart, are you coming over?" she asked.

"Yes, so be ready for me when I get there," Darrius said and hung up the phone.

Lizeth looked over at the bedside clock and could see that it was four in the morning and Darrius was still not home. She tried his cell but it kept going to voicemail. Then it stopped going to voicemail because it was now full with messages she left. Where is he? She was trying her best to stay up but her eyes kept closing. "I can't believe he is not home yet! Where could he be?" she said out loud. She tried his cell one last time but it was completely off this time. Lizeth could no longer fight off her sleep and she drifted into a deep sleep. She must have slept through her alarm because when she woke up it was 1:00 in the afternoon. Lizeth looked at her cell phone to see if maybe he called, but there was no missed call from him or any text messages. Lizeth got up and took her a shower. Once she got out and put some clothes on, Darrius was still nowhere in sight. Lizeth was beginning to worry. Nevertheless, that worry soon turned to anger once Darrius finally came through the door.

She was so furious with him that she didn't say anything, she just walked past him and went out the door. She heard the door open and could feel him staring at her, but she didn't turn back around, she just kept walking towards her car. Once she had the key in the door to unlock it she heard the door close. He must have shut the door, she thought. She was just about to get in when a hand pulled her back. She turned around to see that it was Darrius, who clearly looked like he was drinking and god knows what else.

"Li—" Darrius was about to speak.

"No!" Lizeth cut him off, putting one finger up. "I don't

want to hear one word from you." She pushed him away, jumped inside of her car and drove off. Lizeth was on a mission today despite how her day started.

Lizeth went by the old firm she use to work for to see if they had an opening and to her surprise they were more than willing to give her a job there. They said because she was so good they felt that in a year she could be back on track to building up her clientele. Lizeth was so excited to hear that. She then went shopping and got her nails and hair done. Once she was finished pampering herself she went to the grocery store to get groceries. She was enjoying her time away from the house. Darrius was calling her every second he could so she decided to turn off her phone.

When she pulled up back at home, Darrius was already at the door. "Where were you Lizeth?"he shouted.

Lizeth was still pissed at him and decided that she was not going to entertain him. Lizeth continued to retrieve the groceries from the car without saying or looking at Darrius.

"I know you hear me talking to you woman!" Darrius shouted. Lizeth grabbed all the bags she could and brought them inside to the kitchen. Darrius was grabbing bags as well, still yelling and talking mess. Lizeth was in a better mood and she was tuning Darrius out. Once all the bags were in the house, they began putting the things away.

"So you're not going to say anything to me?" Darrius asked. Lizeth still didn't say anything, she just continued with what she was doing.

"Well fuck it," Darrius said. Darrius decided to go to his office and focus on work. Once he got there, the office that was usually full of life with people walking in and out, was half empty. He got onto the elevator and pressed the button to the top floor. The elevator music was so soothing and relaxing. Darrius always enjoyed it. Once the elevator hit the top floor, the doors opened. Darrius stepped out to his floor and he noticed just how nice his office really was. He went into his office to find it neat as always, thanks to Martha. To his surprise, it was not much work on his desk to do.

Darrius had already completed the new club owner's blueprints and faxed them over to him. The owner approved the design and said they can begin on the groundwork some time in a few months. 'Then there was the call he would be receiving from Nelson. Hopefully it's about business and nothing else, Darrius thought. Darrius began looking in his message tray to see if he had any messages and of course, he had a small stack of them. At least this would give me some time to allow Lizeth to calm down before I go back home.

Darrius began calling and handling all the messages so that when Monday came he wouldn't have an overflow of them. Before he knew it, he had finished all his calls and prepared his things for the following week. Darrius shut his computer down and was getting ready to leave when he heard the elevator.

That is weird, he thought. No one should be here and the cleaning people do not come until nightfall. Darrius checked his watch to make sure. It was just past four o'clock. Yeah they don't come till ten o'clock. Darrius got up and headed towards the door, but on the floor he noticed a piece of paper. He picked up the paper and it was a note addressed to him that read, "What goes around comes around Darrius."

What the hell is this? he wondered, looking around. His first thought was Nelson Carter. Darrius took the note and placed it in his pocket for evidence so he could show it to Mr. Carter and let him know that he does not play these types of games. Who the hell does he think he is?

He walked to the elevator and once there his mind went blank and his body went stiff. On the elevator door was a pair of lips in the shape of a kiss in red lipstick with the message, "What goes around comes around Darrius."He shook his head and chuckled. Somebody is playing games.

Chapter 4

Darrius initially thought it was Nelson leaving those notes, but after the meeting they had a few months ago he was not sure anymore of who sent the note or wrote on the elevator. A few months had gone by since Darrius first received that weird note in his office and the writing on the elevator. Since then he had received random things here and there. There were pictures of him going about his day, along with pictures of him in provocative positions with some random woman he had on the side. Along with that, things between him and Lizeth seem to be getting back to normal. They came to a decision that she was able to return to work and he had begun working alongside Nelson.

Darrius still wanted to keep it a 'professional only'

relationship, but eventually they started hanging out outside of business. Darrius found it weird how close he felt to Nelson, as if they were two of the same. Nelson even offered to help him find out who was really behind the notes and pictures. Darrius thought it would only be fair since he accused Nelson of being the culprit in the first place. Some would think that the two were more than just business partners, but longtime friends. Which at this point is what they were becoming. Darrius was hard at work when Martha walked into his office with a package that came for him.

"Mr. Jackson, the delivery person left this for you," Martha said, placing the box onto his desk. Darrius looked up at the box that had no address on it.

"Martha, do you see something wrong with this box?" he asked her.

"No sir, I do not," she answered.

"Well allow me to point it out for you," Darrius said in a condescending tone. "There is no return address! Did you forget what the office procedure is for mail or deliveries without a return address?"

"I apologize," Martha said. "It was at my desk when I came back from lunch," she added.

"Well just get rid of it," Darrius said as he looked back

down to his work. It seemed that whoever was doing this was taking it up a notch. They would call his phone with just breathing and continue to call him up at work. Darrius had an automated service placed on the phone lines so that whoever it was would not keep the phone lines tied up. It was working out just fine until the voicemail systems would be full of messages with only breathing. Darrius was really annoyed with this and wanted to find out soon who was behind it all.

Darrius noticed that his phone line was beeping red, indicating that he had a phone call on hold.

"Mr. Jackson," Martha buzzed in. "You have a call on line one."

"I see, so who is it?" Darrius asked.

"He said not to tell you," Martha said hesitantly. Immediately Darrius picked up the phone and being shouting into the receiver.

"This is my business and my life, I don't have time for your nonsense! What's with all the letters, notes and pic---."

"What the hell are you talking about Darrius?" the male voice interrupted. Instantly Darrius caught his brother's voice. "Man what's going on? Are you in trouble?" he asked.

"Oh no man, it's just work related," Darrius lied. "How are you doing Travis? It's been a long time." Travis was

Darrius' oldest brother, they were very close growing up.

Travis took pride in being an older brother. He would always look out for Darrius no matter what it was, even though they had a big age difference. Travis was 49 and Darrius was 37, but that didn't matter to Travis, he always treated him as an equal.

Once Travis got married, he did not hear much from him, which Darrius understood as married life is a job of its own. "I was checking up on my little brother and all is ok with me," Travis said.

"That's good to hear," Darrius said. "So tell me, what is new with you? When are you coming to visit me?" Darrius asked excitedly.

"Well I was calling you so you would know that I will be coming your way in about a week and if it was okay if I stay with you when I touch down?" Travis asked.

"That would be fine, me and Lizeth would love to have you man, you know you're more than welcome," Darrius said.

"Cool. Cool," Travis said. Darrius could sense that his brother had more to say but was not saying it.

"Travis is everything okay?" Darrius asked.

"Yeah man, everything is cool. Look, I don't want to

hold you up, but I will call you again when I get there," Travis said.

"Okay," Darrius said.

"Alright bro, see you in a few days," Travis said.

"Alright, talk to you soon," Darrius said and ended the call. What is going on with Travis? Darrius wondered. He looked down at his watch and noticed it was time for lunch.

*****

Wow, what a rush that was! Lizeth thought as she walked out the courtroom. Being back to doing what she loved was great. She had been working non-stop since she got back into practicing law. She had calls coming in from everyone wanting her to represent them due to her father's reputation, along with her making a name for herself as well. Some of the calls were just people in general congratulating her on her come back, but most of them were people needing her services. As much as she enjoyed all the attention, only the best of the best cases would get her something her father taught her, and all the small ones would go to a fresh out of school lawyer.

Lizeth was on cloud nine, she was just so happy. She got

a call at her office from Darrius wanting to meet with her for lunch, which she agreed to as the terms to their compromise. Their lunch hours would be spent together, which has been kept without any interruptions on both ends. Today they were meeting at a nice Italian restaurant called Travinia. Lizeth loved this restaurant, their food was always fresh and the service was great.

When she walked inside of the restaurant Darrius was already sitting at a table. He stood once he noticed her with a smile on his face as she approached.

"Good afternoon Mrs. Jackson," Darrius smiled, giving her a hug and kiss. Lizeth smiled as Darrius pulled her chair out.

"Good Afternoon Mr. Jackson."

"So how was your day?" Darrius asked her once he took his seat.

"My day was great as always," Lizeth responded.

"That's good to hear," Darrius said.

"So how was your day?" she asked him.

"It was good," Darrius said, still smiling at his wife.

"Why are you smiling so hard?" Lizeth asked.

"You're beautiful," he said. Lizeth smiled and blushed. As of late Darrius had been trying to be supportive of her, rather than demanding to do things. Lizeth was enjoying this but she still could not help but feel that he thought she should not be working. However, she never let on that she felt that way.

"We should order something," Lizeth suggested. They both picked up their menus and looked them over. Darrius motioned for the waiter to come and take their orders. They did not have to wait too long before their food arrived, which was why Lizeth loved this place. They finish their meal and exited the restaurant.

"Travis called me at work today," Darrius said as he and Lizeth were walking to their cars.

"He did, how is he doing?" Lizeth asked.

"I think he is okay for the most part," he said.

"What do you mean most part?" she asked, now standing by her car door.

"He just seemed different," he said.

"Oh, I do hope everything is alright with him," she said with concern.

"Well I will find out in a week, he is supposed to visit with us," he said.

"That would be great. I know you would enjoy that," Lizeth smiled. Darrius walked around to Lizeth, pulled her face into his and kissed her long and passionately.

He then pulled away slowly and just looked into her eyes for a moment. Lizeth could feel herself getting wet and she knew if she acted on it, she would not make it back into work.

"How about we take the rest of the day off," Darrius suggested, still staring into her eyes.

"Uh, okay," Lizeth stuttered. Darrius smiled, backed up and opened her car door for her.

"I will see you at home," Darrius said.

"Not if I get there first," Lizeth said with a big smile on her face. They both got into their cars and met up at home.

"Yes...Yes...Yesss!" Lizeth screamed as Darrius hit it from behind.

"You like that?" Darrius grunted, smacking her on her ass.

"Yesssss," Lizeth moaned. Darrius loved the way she sounded when she moaned, it drove him crazy. Darrius pulled her hands behind her back as if he was about to handcuff her and lifted off the bed with nothing but her knees touching the bed. In this position he had total control of how deep he could go. Darrius then pulled her back as he went forward into her pussy. He could hear how wet she was from the gushing sound of every thrust. The deeper he went the louder she got.

Darrius was feeling like a wild man. Her sounds were driving him insane, giving him the strength to go on for a long time.

Oh my goodness, the things he is doing to me! Lizeth thought to herself. With each thrust she could feel herself about to explode. He would go deeper and deeper, then slow down to a grinding circular motion.

"Ahh...fuck girl, see what you do to me!" Darrius shouted over Lizeth's moans. Darrius stopped and pushed Lizeth down on her stomach, kissing her all over her back and all over her ass.

"Oh... Yes...," Lizeth moaned. He took his erect penis out of her ass and flipped her over onto her back. Then he took his tongue and shoved it down her throat. While he grabbed her breasts, Lizeth was in pure ecstasy. Darrius took his tongue from her mouth to her neck and worked it all the way down to her stomach and onto her clitoris. He moved his tongue in a circular motion, then up and down. He could feel her getting aroused again. Each time he would lick, she would move as if she was trying to get away.

Darrius took his hands and interlocked them so that

Lizeth could not move. He then started to spell the alphabets over her whole vagina and it made her go wild. He could feel her orgasm approaching as her body started to shake, and eating her pussy was making his dick harder. Her aroma was so intoxicating. He got up and in one motion put his hard dick inside of her wet pussy and they both came simultaneously. Darrius collapsed on top of Lizeth, both breathing heavily until they both fell into a deep sleep.

Lizeth woke up to the sound of the shower running. She glanced over to the bedside clock and notice that it was midnight. Lizeth smiled and got up to join Darrius in the shower.

She walked in and just stood as she looked at her handsome husband in the shower. There he stood, all 6'3 of him. She admired his athletic build. Lizeth had to admit that she was enjoying the view. She walked over, opened the door, and walked in. She placed her hands around his waist and kissed him on his back.

"Oh, so you're awake now?" Darrius grinned.

"Yes, but I could of slept forever. However, I think I have something else in mind," she smiled seductively. Darrius could feel her smiling from behind him.

He turned to face her. "Is that right?" he said. Lizeth

smiled and kissed him on his chest. "Don't start something woman," Darrius warned her. Lizeth kissed him on his chest again. She kissed him all over his abdomen, slid to her knees and kissed the tip of his dick.

"Uhmm," Darrius groaned. Lizeth then grabbed his massive dick with both her hands. She began to stroke it and lick it. She then put the head of his penis in her mouth and started sucking it. Damn this feels good, Darrius thought to himself as he watched his wife gave him a wet head job.

She was sucking it so hard and doing this trick with her tongue. She took his entire dick in her mouth and Darrius could feel his knees get weak. She must have felt it to because her sucking intensified. Darrius could feel a powerful nut approaching. Before he knew it, he came all in her mouth and she swallowed every bit of it. Darrius fell back against the shower tile to try to compose himself so he wouldn't lose his balance. Lizeth stood to her feet, gave him a devious smile then began to shower. Darrius did not want to feel defeated so once he got his self together he grabbed Lizeth from behind and shoved him dick inside of her already moist pussy. Oh yeah I got that ass now, Darrius thought with a big grin on his face.

72

*****

Lizeth was slammed with work and not only that, she got up rather late. She slept through her alarm but once she got to work she got into the flow of things. She began working on case files that she had and she was surprisingly focused until the secretary walked in to let her know that she had a call on line two. It must be Darrius. She picked up the phone. "Lizeth Jackson speaking, may I help you."

"Lizeth we need to talk," the female voice said. Lizeth hung the phone up. She knew the voice on the other end was Sam. She had been calling her job for the last few days and each time Lizeth would hang up the phone. Sam had not spoken to her or reached out to her in a while now and each time she tried to call her she got the voicemail. Lizeth was not even sure how Sam found out that she was back working because only a few people knew. However, she didn't really care.

Lizeth could hear her cell phone vibrate in her desk drawer. She opened it to see that it was a pop up from the app she downloaded called Blacklist. She had downloaded the app to prevent Sam from calling or texting her phone. She hadn't spoken to Sam since that night at her house. Lizeth tried calling Sam on many occasions but could not reach her on the phone. Since she was acting strange, Lizeth decided to give her a taste of her own medicine. At this point, Lizeth was over it and did not want to hear from her at all. Lizeth spent most of her time focusing on her work. It has been taking up most of her time so not speaking to Sam for a while could have partially been her fault, but Lizeth felt she could do without the drama being that the last time they did speak Sam made her feel rather uncomfortable.

*****

Darrius received a call from Martha that he may need to come into the office. He had late meetings scheduled for the day that would keep him from having to go to the office early, but because of how Martha sounded on the phone he made a trip to the office. When he got there, he could tell that Martha looked worried.

"Martha what's going on?" Darrius asked. Martha looked as if she was about to cry.

"Mr. Jackson I am so sorry to have to tell you this," Martha said.

"Tell me what Martha," Darrius responded with

apprehension in his voice.

"I have misplaced or lost the file that contained personal information on you and your clients, past and present, along with the staff," Martha whispered with tears in her eyes.

Darrius' eyes widened and his jaws tightened. "How the hell did that happen Martha?"Darrius shouted hysterically. "That information is not supposed to leave the office anyway, so how can it get lost? It's supposed to be locked up anyway!" Darrius added. Darrius was so loud that other people came out of their offices.

"Mr. Jackson, that is not all," Martha alleged.

"What do you mean?" Darrius asked, throwing his hands up.

"Mr. Jackson, I really think we should go into your office for what I need to tell you," Martha said.

"Why?' Darrius asked.

"Mr. Jackson please," Martha begged, gesturing towards his office.

Darrius just stood shaking his head and rubbing the back of his neck. "Fine," he muttered.

They walked to his office and Martha followed behind nervously. Darrius went and sat on his desk as Martha walked in with her head down and her hands interlocked.

"Should we close the door?" Darrius asked impatiently. As Martha turned to close the door she could see her fellow co-workers standing around looking. She turned to face Darrius who was sitting on the edge of his desk with his arms folded across his chest, looking directly at her with rage in his eyes. "Martha get on with it," Darrius said with a tight jaw.

"Well not only did I misplace or lose the file, but---," Martha began but stopped.

"Stop dragging this shit out!" Darrius yelled.

"I am not sure how long the file has been missing," Martha blurted out.

Darrius could feel his blood pressure rising and his temper flaring. He was getting so distressed that he became belligerent. He picked up one of his office chairs and threw it across the room. Martha was so afraid that she ran into a corner with her hands over her head. "Martha, how in the hell!" Darrius shouted.

"Sir, I am so sorry," Martha apologized. "I usually would check the file each week, but we have been so busy lately," Martha pleaded to him.

"So when did you realize it was gone?" Darrius asked.

"I only noticed it today because of the work you're

doing with Mr. Carter," Martha said.

"Do you know what that means, or do you realize what could happen if that information gets out?" Darrius asked her.

"Yes, sir I do," Martha said, now coming out of the corner. Darrius had to compose his self and calm down. He started to pace the floor, thinking of what steps he needed to take.

"First thing we need to do is get in contact with everyone and inform them of what happened," Darrius said.

"Mr. Jackson shouldn't we wait? I may find it," Martha said.

"No! It's best we inform everyone just in case something comes up."

"Yes sir, you're right," Martha nodded.

"So, I need you to type up a memo to all employees as well as send out emails and letters to anyone we have worked with," Darrius said.

"Yes sir," Martha said as she turned to head for the door.

"Make sure I approve it all before you send it out," Darrius said. As Martha walked out Darrius sat in his big office chair and stared at the ceiling, thinking on how much of a mess this will soon become. Not only is he getting stalked from some random person, but now his business was headed for big trouble.

Darrius closed his eyes and just remembered the good times. He tried to think where he went wrong but nothing came to mind. At that very moment his computer made a sound, indicating he had an email. There is no way she typed that memo up that quickly, he thought. Darrius entered his password to unlock his screen and clicked on his email box icon.

One of the email's subject lines caught his eye. It read: MISSING FILE. That can't be a right, he thought. He clicked on the email and once it opened, there in the attachment was the file he and Martha were just discussing with the words, LOOKING FOR ME? written at the bottom. "What the hell?" Darrius said as he put his hand over his mouth. It was at that point he realized that this just got serious.

Chapter 5

"Yo, what's up bro.?" Darrius said as he opened his door to welcome his brother in.

"Hey man," Travis said as he walked inside, placed his suitcase down and gave Darrius a hug.

"Sorry about not showing up last week man, things got hectic for me," Travis said.

"Man it's okay, just a pleasure to see you," Darrius said as he led his brother into the living room.

"So how is everything going for you?" Travis asked as he sat down on the sofa.

"Well its going okay," Darrius lied again, not wanting to speak on what was actually going on at work.

"That doesn't sound to convincing man. You okay?" Travis asked.

"Yeah, it's nothing I can't handle," Darrius said, trying to sound more convincing, but it was clear from his brother's face that he was not buying it.

"Darrius let me know what's going on with you. I can tell something is up," Travis said.

"Enough about me. What about you, what's going on with you?" Darrius asked, trying to change the subject.

"Okay, so you're still avoiding the question," Travis said with a slight laugh.

"It's not that, I just---," Darrius began, but Lizeth walked into the living room.

"Hi Travis," Lizeth said as she walked over to give him a hug.

"Hi how are you?" Travis said.

"I am good. It's so good to see you," Lizeth said.

"Glad to hear it. I was just telling Darrius that I am sorry I was not able to make it like I planned to last week," Travis apologized.

"That's ok. Well, I don't want to interrupt you two," Lizeth said as she walked over to Darrius and gave him a long and passionate kiss.

"Damn bra!" Travis chuckled as he looked on at the two.

"Whatever," Darrius mumbled jokingly.

"I will be in the kitchen working on some stuff, just call me if you need me," Lizeth said as she walked out the living room towards the kitchen.

Lizeth walked into the kitchen with a sigh of relief. She thought she was caught. She thought that Darrius was still out on his morning run when she was in his office looking around for something earlier that day and she came across a note that read:

What goes around, comes around Darrius

This note led her to believe that something was going on that he was not telling, or trying to keep from her. Either way, she wanted to know what was going on and it was clear he was not talking about it.

Lizeth managed to get his suitcase open and that was when she discovered pictures of him and other women and more letters along with emails. What the hell? Many emotions and thoughts were running through her head. He was cheating on her with multiple women. The more she looked at the pictures the angrier she became. She had to hold her tears in as she looked at the pictures. She was just about to take all of them when she heard Darrius and someone talking downstairs. Lizeth wanted answers, but she did not want to bring it to Darrius' attention that she knew so she decided to go and visit Martha today before she went into work to get answers on both the notes and emails, in addition to the women in the pictures. With Darrius distracted by his brother, this would be the perfect time.

"Damn man I can't believe you're going through all this," Travis said in response to Darrius finally telling him about what was going on at work.

"Yeah, it's just getting out of control," Darrius said, shaking his head."I have a person looking into it though," he added.

"That's good. Do you have any idea who it could be?" Travis asked.

"At this point I don't have a clue," Darrius said.

"Can I ask you a question?" Travis said, sounding more serious than before.

"Sure man, ask me anything," Darrius said.

"What made you want to mess around on your wife.?" Travis asked.

"To be honest, I don't really know. At the time I didn't care and I felt it was okay," Darrius admitted.

"Cheating on your wife is never okay," Travis scolded.

"It's not like she is going to find out," Darrius said.

"Well looks like she may," Travis said.

"I doubt it. She works now, she's too busy," Darrius said.

"You come off like it's not that big of a deal," Travis said.

"How, and why you pressing this man?" Darrius said, now getting upset.

"You're doing the same shit dad did to mom and you should know better!" Travis yelled.

Darrius felt like he was just punched in the stomach. All he could see was flashes of his childhood appearing and none of them looked as if his mother was hurting or his father had cheated.

"Watch your damn mouth. Our father did not cheat on our mother!" Darrius said as he stood to his feet.

"Really? They said you wouldn't remember being that you had to go to a therapist because you couldn't handle it then," Travis said as he stood and walked towards Darrius.

"Is this the reason you came, so you could tell me some bullshit?" Darrius asked.

"No, I came because I needed to talk to you on why you haven't heard from me in a while," Travis said, now sounding sad.

"Travis what's going on man? I knew something was up

from the moment you were on the phone," Darrius said, quickly calming down. Both men sat back down and Darrius looked at his brother whose eyes began to water. Travis looked down at the floor and stated to talk.

"I really screwed things up in my marriage," Travis said.

"What?" Darrius asked, stunned.

"Let me finish," Travis said.

"Everything was good in the beginning. We got along and I was happy with her. Somehow along the way I found myself wanting the company of other women. It was good and I loved it. She did not know and at some point, I did not care. I got so caught up in it that I failed to even notice my wife was leaving me. Hell, when I realized it she was already gone," Travis said with tears now coming from his eyes.

"Man I am so sorry, I didn't know you were dealing with this," Darrius said.

"Well, there is more," Travis said through sniffs. "After she left everything just kind of hit me all at once. I started drinking, and then gambling became an issue for me," Travis confessed, now sobbing. "I lost everything!" Travis said in between sobs.

"Hey man, it's going to be alright," Darrius said as he

hugged his brother.

"No man, it's not going to be alright," Travis said as he pushed away from Darrius and got up from the seat. "Don't you see, we are cursed!" Travis shouted out.

"What do you mean cursed?" Darrius said jokingly.

"You think this shit funny?" Travis said.

"No man, but you sounding crazy as hell. You messed up, so what?" Darrius shrugged.

"Crazy? Not at all. My ex-wife is expecting a child," Travis said.

"That's good to hear man, congrats," Darrius said.

Travis just stood in silence and turned his head away from him. "It's not mine," Travis said softly.

"I am so sorry bra," Darrius said.

"I just don't want you to go through what I went through man," Travis said. "You may not believe me about dad, but I didn't know about you cheating on your wife until now, and you just found out about what I did to mine. So, if that is not enough to prove to you, just go and visit the folks. We just repeating the same shit he did to mom," Travis said.

"Enough with that, our actions are our own, not dad's," Darrius said.

"Maybe you're right, but one thing I know is I allowed

my pride and the fact that I am a man get in the way of what was most important," Travis said as he turned back around to face Darrius.

"And what was that?" Darrius asked.

"Making sure my wife stayed happy," Travis said.

"Well my wife is not going anywhere," Darrius said.

"Yeah let's hope so. One of us got to get it right," Travis responded.

*****

Lizeth sat in her car in front of Darrius' company thinking of how to go about getting information from Martha without coming off as though she is clueless. I will just go in there and demand answers, Lizeth thought to herself. No that would be too direct. Oh well, nothing like the present, she thought as she got out of her car and started walking towards the building. The good thing about not being seen up here often made it easy for her to be excused as a normal person. Once she was on the elevator, two other people were discussing an email that came out talking about a leak where someone could have obtained personal information.

As she listened to the two on the elevator talk, they

began talking about filing a potential lawsuit against the company. So it's deeper than I thought, Lizeth thought as she listened on. The conversation came to a complete stop once the doors to the elevator opened and the two got off. She wondered if she should follow them. She quickly recanted her thoughts to follow and remained on the elevator because she did not want to risk missing Martha. The elevator doors closed and Lizeth stood back and waited for it to reach the top. The elevator kept going up until it reached its desired floor, the doors opened and Lizeth stepped out. To her surprise, Martha was standing at her desk as if she was already waiting on her. Martha waved her over. Lizeth walked over to Martha who seemed to look as if she was stressed.

"Is everything okay Martha?" Lizeth asked.

"Mrs. Jackson, I have been trying to reach your husband all day," Martha said, sounding frantic.

"Martha please calm down and tell me what's going on," Lizeth said. As Lizeth sat down with Martha she listened to Martha explain everything that was going on in the office. How she misplaced a file and had to send out the memo to all employees and clients, past and present. She also informed her about all the mysterious emails and letters along with packages that had been coming to the office for Darrius.

After Martha finished telling her this, she looked as if she was relieved, but that moment passed rather quickly once the phone started ringing again. As Martha informed her of all the recent happenings, Lizeth was trying to think of who to call to help save her husband, despite his cheating ways. She started grilling Martha with questions to get to the truth.

"So Martha, who do you think could behind all this?" Lizeth asked.

"I am not sure," Martha answered.

"Has anyone recently got fired?" Lizeth asked.

"No, no one's been fired. I would have to handle that paper work," Martha told her.

"Did he have an argument with someone or upset someone?" Lizeth asked.

"No I don't think so," Martha said.

"Okay, well that gets us nowhere!" Lizeth sighed, clearly frustrated.

"Sorry I can't be more help," Martha apologized.

"Well who would have access to this information other than you?" Lizeth grilled her.

"No one," Martha said.

"Well no one got fired, so did anyone get hired here

recently?" Lizeth asked.

"Well, no new hires. All we had was an intern who was from the college, but Mr. Jackson all of a sudden chose to end the program with the school," Martha said.

"Why did he do that?" Lizeth asked curiously.

"According to Mr. Jackson, she was getting too attached here and she was not really working out," Martha explained. Lizeth felt as if she had just found the piece to the puzzle but was still not sure.

"So do you think she could be behind this?" Lizeth asked.

"Well when she was escorted off the property she didn't seem at all upset," Martha said.

"She was escorted off the property?" Lizeth asked.

"Yes, Mr. Jackson thought it best," Martha said.

"Now that you mention it, she did get to work with me once or twice, but I don't think that she would do this," Martha said.

Lizeth was sure that this intern was behind this, and she planned on finding out the truth.

"Martha if I wanted to find an intern or this intern for my company how would I go about doing so?" Lizeth asked.

"Well the college is a good choice, they have such bright

students. But if you want to speak with that particular intern I have her information here," Martha said as she went into her desk and pulled out a folder with 'Jessica Jones' printed on it. "You can't look in it, only I can," Martha said.

"I understand," Lizeth nodded.

"That's weird," Martha said.

"What?" Lizeth asked.

"Her folder is completely empty," Martha said. Both women sat in silence looking at one another.

"Well I don't want to keep you from your work," Lizeth said, getting up to leave.

"It was nice to talk to you Mrs. Jackson. Again, I am sorry about our mix-up before."

"Tell you what, if you can keep this conversation between me and you I will forget about that mix-up," Lizeth said as she smiled.

"My lips are sealed," Martha promised as she gestured zipping her lips.

Lizeth was not too sure if that was really the case, but she hoped she held up to her word. She did not need her husband to know that she was well aware of what was going on. She could not ask Martha about the women in the pictures being that she was already dealing with so much already. Lizeth entered the elevator and pulled out her cell phone.

"Hi, this is Lizeth Jackson I will need for you to set up a meeting with me and the partners. I have reason to believe that my husband's business is being sabotaged and I will need their support on this," Lizeth spoke into her phone.

"Will do," the voice on the other end said.

"Good. Call me with the details," Lizeth said as she exited the elevator.

"She must have gone for a run," Darrius said to Travis as they walked into the kitchen.

"That's good, got to stay healthy," Travis said. "So what are your plans for today?" Travis asked.

"I just have to call into work and see what my secretary wanted. She's been calling me non-stop," Darrius said, looking down to his phone.

"Maybe it's important, you should call her back," Travis advised.

"You're right, can't avoid it forever," Darrius said as his phone started to ring. "I got to take this," Darrius told Travis, pointing to his phone.

"Man go ahead, I will be alright," Travis said. Once Darrius left the room Travis could hear him on the phone

91

with who he figured to be his secretary.

Darrius was asking her questions about how many and how long. Then there was a moment of silence, and then he could hear Darrius say that it looked as if they had no choice but to make it public. Travis could tell by his voice that he was frustrated. Darrius soon walked back into the kitchen to join his brother with a look of horror on his face.

"Man, it's not looking good for my company and at this rate even my marriage might be in trouble," Darrius said as he dropped his head into his hands.

"Listen to what you just said. You're about to lose your company and your wife," Travis said knowingly.

"Travis man, right now is not the time man," Darrius said, looking up.

"I can't help that despite all that is going on you still got messed up priorities," Travis said.

"What are you talking about?" Darrius asked with agitation in his voice.

"You man! Your wife should be the first thing you should be concerned with losing, fuck the business!" Travis said with hostility in his voice.

"I worked hard for my business!" Darrius yelled.

"Well if you worked that damn hard in your marriage

maybe this shit wouldn't be happening," Travis shot back.

"What the hell you mean by that? I do what I am supposed to in my marriage," Darrius said angrily as he walked up on his brother.

"First of all bra, you didn't do what you was supposed to in your marriage, you did what you wanted to," Travis corrected him as he pushed Darrius back up off him. Darrius was about to hit his brother but he had to calm himself down.

"You don't know what the hell you're talking about. Not my fault I can handle my business better than you, so how about you get out my house!" Darrius yelled.

"Wow! You are really something, I can't believe you man. Regardless, I will still pray for you cause you're going to need it," Travis said, sounding hurt.

Travis walked out of the kitchen to grab his things and Darrius followed behind, quickly regretting the things he said. Travis picked up his suitcase and walked to the door. As he was about to walk out, he stopped and turned around to face Darrius.

"Oh yeah, the purpose of this visit was for me to tell you something you needed to know," Travis said.

"What is that?" Darrius asked.

"Tell me this, did you know we had another brother?"

Travis asked, staring at Darrius before walking out and slamming the door behind him.

Darrius stood staring at the door trying to comprehend what had just transpired with him and his brother. Darrius had so much going on that he refused to accept anything that Travis said. He felt he might be saying those things only because he is down and going through some things. Whatever the reason, Darrius was determined to look past it and focus on what was going on around him; and that was saving his business as well as his marriage.

****

Darrius was still stunned from the information his brother had given him. When Lizeth came home and asked where he was Darrius told her he had to leave for some emergency. Lizeth told him that it was weird because Travis called her and told her about the fight they had. Darrius never lied to Lizeth, but with so much going on he found himself doing all kinds of things. With all that was going on with his company and being stalked, Darrius started to drink heavier to ease some of the stress, which caused him to end up with random women. He was also visiting the bar more than he was returning home.

At one point he even started staying away from home. He would leave work and end up in a bar and soon wake up in some random woman's bed. Darrius felt lost as if he was losing control. He was already being threatened by clients that they were going to sue him, along with many of his employees wanting to quit if the situation was not properly handled.

When Darrius got to work today it seemed as if it was a normal workday. He was not getting ugly looks from any of his employees as he did the previous weeks. Once he reached his floor even Martha seemed to be less frantic than before. She even greeted him and informed him that he had a few messages, but none concerning the leak. He was not sure what was happening, but he was going to enjoy this breath of fresh air. Nelson was sitting in his office as he walked in.

"Nelson, how are you doing?" Darrius asked as he walked over to greet him.

"I am okay, I was coming to see how you were?" Nelson said.

"It's been hell man," Darrius admitted.

"Well it may get better," Nelson said.

"Should I close the door?" Darrius asked.

"I will," Nelson said as he walked over and closed the door.

"You found something?" Darrius asked with relief in his eyes.

"Yes. We have reason to believe that the person behind this is not someone who is working here," Nelson informed him.

"So who is it?" Darrius asked.

"I don't want to tell you just yet, I want to be absolutely sure that it is this woman," Nelson said.

"So it's a woman?" Darrius asked.

"Yes and that is all I will tell you," Nelson said firmly. Darrius understood and left it alone. "Just know you will be the first to know once it's confirmed. So don't do anything or start trying to guess who it is, just focus on your work," Nelson said.

"You're right, I will do just that. In fact, we should set up a meeting for us to discuss the design of the building," Darrius suggested.

"There's no need to discuss. I already approved it. Despite your personal life, you're good at what you do," Nelson said, assuring Darrius that he trusted his decision on the project.

"Thank you for that," Nelson said.

"Well I have a meeting to get to," Nelson said.

"Okay, I'll walk you to the elevator," Darrius said.

"How is your wife doing by the way?" Nelson asked.

Darrius' eyes went wide as a deer caught in headlights. He had not seen his wife in over a week, at the least. The past few weeks were a blur for him. He was still getting over a hangover from last night.

"Darrius man, did you hear me?" Nelson asked.

"Ah yeah man, I heard you. She is doing fine, she's been busy with work," Darrius said.

"Okay, if you say so," Nelson said as he got onto the elevator. Nelson gave Darrius a look of uncertainty as the elevator doors closed and descended to the lower lobby.

"Martha I need you to order me some flowers and send them to my wife's job," Darrius said as he wrote down Lizeth's job address and a special message to be included with the flowers.

"Yes sir will do," Martha said as she took the address and called the nearest florist in the city. Darrius walked back to his office and closed his office door. He sat down at his desk and just recalled the last few months and even his actions over the years. What am I doing? he asked himself..

Darrius started to think about his brother and that maybe he should call him and apologize. Rather than think on it any longer, Darrius picked up his phone and dialed his brother's number.

*****

"He sent you flowers," Lizeth's dinky secretary said as she brought the large bouquet of flowers to her desk. Lizeth was not impressed with the flowers that Darrius had sent. She has not seen him as much lately and even when he was home it was as if he was not there.

"Well since you like them so much how about you take them?" Lizeth said.

"Are you serious?" she asked with a look of surprise.

"Yes I am. Take them so I can get ready for my meeting," Lizeth said, waving her off.

"Okay, what about the card?" she said as she held the card in her hand.

"Easy, give it to me," Lizeth said as she took the card and put it in the shredder without giving it a glance. Her secretary stood in disbelief.

"Please don't stand there. Take the flowers and get back

to work, thank you," Lizeth said as she continued to work.

"Yes indeed. I will let you know when Mr. Carter has arrived," she said as she picked up the flowers and went back to her desk.

"What is the purpose of this meeting?" Lizeth asked Nelson as they walked to her conference room.

"I assure you this is not a social visit Mrs....Lizeth," Nelson said.

"Then what is this?" she asked as they sat down to a large, cherry wood table that sat in the center of the conference room surrounded by glass on both sides. The table had at least twenty high back soft wood chairs around it.

"As you know, me and your husband have become rather close lately," Nelson began.

"I'm well aware of this. In fact, I am sure you have seen more of my husband than me," Lizeth said.

"Yes, I just saw him today," Nelson admitted.

"Okay," Lizeth said nonchalantly.

"Well to get to the point, I see that we have a common goal," Nelson told her.

"What's that? Lizeth asked.

"Finding who is after your husband. Only thing is, I

think you already know," Nelson stated.

Lizeth stared at Nelson, trying to figure out what his angle was and where he was going with this. She was well aware of her husband's scandal at work, along with him cheating on her. What she could not figure out was what Nelson's part in all of this was.

Chapter 6

"How do you know this?" Lizeth asked.

"The same way you know all that you do," Nelson said.

"So, you have your sources as well," Lizeth said.

"Yes I do, I need them in my line of work. I think in this case I should just let you have this," Nelson said.

"Why?" Lizeth asked.

"Darrius needs you," Nelson said.

"Ha-ha, that's funny," Lizeth chuckled.

"How is that funny?" Nelson asked.

"You know just as well as I do about my husband's lifestyle outside of our marriage," Lizeth stated, thinking about all the photos of him with those different women.

"He is lost," Nelson spoke, interrupting her from her

thoughts.

Even though she wanted to yell and scream, Lizeth did not allow her emotions to get the best of her. She knew that what Nelson was saying was true.

"That's all I have to say," Nelson said. "I'm sure we will speak again," he added as he got up to leave. "One last question," Nelson said, sitting back down.

"And what is that?" Lizeth asked.

"How are you able to help him, even when you know all that you do?" Nelson asked.

"At the end of the day, he is still my husband and our vows said through for better or worse," Lizeth answered.

Nelson nodded his head in agreement and got up to leave. What's already understood did not need to be discussed any further.

*****

Darrius felt better that he was able to smooth things over with his brother. He felt his brother was only trying to look out for him and at the same time, warn him before he lost it all. After talking to him he decided that it would be best if he told Lizeth everything, regardless of the consequences, but he was still contemplating how he was going to tell her. Darrius was feeling more relaxed today, the most relaxed he had been in a while. That is, until he got an email alert from the strange email address as before. When Darrius read the subject line, he tensed up because he knew who it was from. The subject line read: DID YOU MISS ME.

Darrius continued to read the email that demanded that he have $250,000 cash in a duffel bag ready for pick up at a set location in 48 hours. If the demands were not met, then they would release the information to willing parties. Darrius was beginning to feel as if everything was deteriorating all around him.

*****

Lizeth knew the day was going to come that she would have to speak to Sam again, but after being so long since they last spoke she dismissed it. Well today, she had no choice but to talk to her because she was standing by her car as she walked out of her office building.

"We need to talk," Sam said as Lizeth walked up.

"No you need to talk, I will listen," Lizeth corrected her.

"Well your husband is a scum bag," Sam blurted out.

"Is that right?" Lizeth said, her eyebrows raised.

"Yes. He is a no good asshole and I believe a girl I know was dealing with him for a while," Sam said.

"So who is she?" Lizeth asked.

"I can't give you that information. Just trust me, it would be best that you leave that asshole," Sam advised, putting her hand on her hip.

"Enough," Lizeth said.

"Hey, I'm just trying to look out for you," Sam said with an arrogant tone.

"Let me tell you something. First off, you do not approach me and start talking bad about my husband, no matter how you may feel about him," Lizeth told her, pointing her fingers in Sam's face. Sam tried to talk but Lizeth quickly hushed her with a hand motion. "Second, I haven't seen you or talked to you in almost a month and when I did try to reach out to you, I could never reach you!" Lizeth said with aggression in her voice. "And third, when you do finally pop up, you talking bad about my husband!" Lizeth yelled with fury in her voice.

Sam again tried to speak but Lizeth put up her hand. "You say you looking out for me, but will not give me a name. You say you're a friend but you clearly have not been one. How do I know you're not making this up?" Lizeth asked her. "Your word is about as real as you, and at this point you look fake as hell! I don't know what it is but something is not right with you," Lizeth said, bumping Sam out of her way as she got into her car.

As Lizeth was pulling out, she could see Sam in her review mirror still standing there looking as if she lost her best friend and in Lizeth's mind she did, because Sam was just a little too late. Lizeth drove home contemplating everything that had been happening the last few months and she was just overwhelmed with it all.

The tears were coming down her face in streams and she could not hold it all in anymore. She knew she needed this. Lizeth cried the entire ride home, she got out all her pain in hurt in those tears. When she pulled up into her driveway, she felt much better that she was able to cry out some of the hurt and frustration. She looked in her mirror and fixed her face up before she got out of her car. Surprisingly, Darrius' car was in the driveway, but she didn't want him to see her upset.

As Lizeth walked in the house, she noticed rose petals on the floors and candles lit in the shape of a heart in the center of her walkway. There was a card sitting in the center of the heart with her name on it. She picked it up and opened it. It read:

Sorry is not enough.

But that is where I will start.

Just know that you

Forever and always

Will have my heart.

Lizeth smiled because it brought back memories of when Darrius would leave her notes expressing how he felt for her. Lizeth got a whiff of what smelled like food cooking, which would be new because Darrius never cooked. In fact, she thought he couldn't cook. She was about to head to the kitchen when something on the card caught her eye. It was an arrow pointing in the direction of the steps. She went to the steps and there was another card with an arrow pointing upstairs, along with rose petals on the steps. She followed all the cards with arrows pointing which led her to their bedroom.

Lizeth could see candlelight flickering from inside her bathroom. On the door hung a robe and a note that said, take me and come inside. Lizeth took the robe and opened the bathroom door. Inside she found Darrius in their large garden sized tub, filled with bubbles with two glasses of champagne in his hand.

"Don't speak, just join me," Darrius spoke.

Lizeth just stood and looked at her husband as flashes of him with other women and his short affair with his intern came into her mind. She felt like running away but she knew her feet wouldn't let her. Lizeth closed her eyes, took in a deep breath and ignored the thoughts running through her head.

This was her husband and she would be here for him no matter what. She opened her eyes to see that Darrius was now standing up in the tub. Here stood her handsome husband with his toned, hard, lean frame. He stood naked with soap running down his six-pack, covering some of his tattoos. Lizeth had to admit her husband was extremely sexy. His massive penis stood hard and ready. Lizeth was in awe and she knew that he knew it. Once her eyes finally made it back to his face he had a devilish grin on his face. Lizeth could feel her legs weakening, she wanted him and badly.

"Should I help you undress?" Darrius asked.

"No I got it," Lizeth said as she began removing her clothes. She got all the way down to her Victoria Secret red lace set. She started to take off her bra when Darrius asked her to stop.

"Just stand there for a minute," Darrius asked. Lizeth did as he asked. Darrius stood soaking wet in the tub, staring at his beautiful wife with her coca-cola frame. The way the red lace looked up against her chocolate skin was just breathtaking. Her breasts, a nice 38C, were perky and peeking through the lace. Darrius licked his lips as if he could taste them already. She had a beautiful flat stomach with a pierced belly button that she got while in college. She had a small waist and her thick thighs and juicy ass complemented her nice frame. Lizeth was thick and solid and Darrius loved her curves. Hell, he loved her.

"Okay, now you may continue," Darrius said.

Lizeth finished getting undressed and Darrius helped her into the bath. She sat with her back against his chest. "You look radiant in this candle light," Darrius murmured in Lizeth's ear.

"So do you," Lizeth said. Darrius poured them both a glass of wine and they sat in silence for a while, just taking in the scenery of the moment.

"I want to apologize for my actions these last few months," Darrius said, breaking the silence. "I have been so distant with you," he added.

"You don't have to apologize to me," Lizeth said. It was

hard for her to say it because the hurt that she felt earlier was beginning to come up.

"I do," Darrius said. He started to think on the blackmail, the emails and all the things that were going on with him. He was about to come clean to Lizeth about it all but she turned around and started to kiss him very seductively.

"No more talking okay," Lizeth whispered, as if she knew what he was about to say.

Darrius could see that his wife had a hint of hurt in her eyes. He wanted to ask her if she was okay, but he choose not to. He began kissing her back. Lizeth straddled Darrius and started to move in a back and forth motion. Darrius rubbed her breasts and took them in his mouth. Lizeth moaned in appreciation. He sucked them hungrily and Lizeth would moan louder each time he would go from one breast to the other. Lizeth started to ride him harder. The passion between the two was so intense that the water was spilling over the top of the tub on to the floor. The mirror and glass that surrounded the tub was now fogged up. Darrius grabbed the nape of Lizeth's neck and pushed her down on him harder.

Lizeth moaned louder with each thrust. She could feel herself coming to her point of exploding. She tried to hold it but her orgasm was so powerful that she dug her nails into

Darrius' back. He moaned as he too was about to cum. Lizeth came and collapsed on top of him. Darrius dropped his head back on to the rim of the tub, panting along with Lizeth as they sat in the tub embraced in each other's arms. The only sound was of their heavy breathing.

Darrius got out of the tub and asked Lizeth to come to the kitchen in five minutes. She got out, lotioned up, and waited five minutes before walking downstairs to find Darrius. Lizeth followed the aroma of smells coming from the kitchen. She walked in to the kitchen only to be directed to the dining room with more arrows. She could see pots on the stove but she did not bother to look inside, instead she continued following the arrows. Sitting at a candle lit dinner for two was Darrius with a smile on his face.

"Please join me Mrs. Jackson," Darrius said, gesturing for her to sit down.

"Sure thing Mr. Jackson," Lizeth smiled. She sat down to dinner and they ate and had normal dinner conversation. They cleaned up the kitchen together and ended the night with a bottle of wine in front of their fireplace relaxing.

The following day Darrius received a call from Nelson stating that it was rather urgent he meet with him. Darrius thought he might have found the woman who was behind everything and all this could finally end. Nelson asked that Darrius meet him at a local Sports bar away from the office so they could talk privately. Darrius agreed to meet him on his lunch break, which he usually reserved for Lizeth, but as of late she has been just as busy as he has.

Darrius pulled up to the Sports bar and walked inside. The smell of fresh fried burgers hit him in the nose. This particular bar was known for their juicy burgers. Darrius planned on getting one after he spoke with Nelson. Darrius spotted Nelson at the bar sitting with a drink in his hand. Nelson noticed Darrius walking up and stood up to greet him.

"Hey," Darrius said as he extended his hand to Nelson's.

"What's up?" Nelson greeted him. "I got something to tell you. I didn't really have anyone else to talk to," Nelson said as both men sat down to the bar.

"It sounds serious man," Darrius said.

"It is," Nelson said with a serious look on his face.

"What's going on?" Darrius asked.

"I just found out that I was adopted," Nelson said in a pained voice. Darrius gave a puzzled look to Nelson.

"What! Are you serious?" Darrius asked. "You're just now finding this out?"

"Yes. My mother, or adopted mother, I don't know what

111

to call her now, told me this just a few hours ago," Nelson said as he gripped the shot of liquor in his hand.

"Why now?" Darrius asked.

"She said she has always wanted to tell me but never could find the right time," Nelson said. "She also said that my father is really sick. My real father," Nelson added.

Darrius was unsure what to say at this moment. This was a lot. What would be the right words in a situation like this? "I honestly don't know what to tell you man," Darrius said.

"I know man, I just needed to talk to somebody," Nelson said.

"I understand man. Seems we can't seem to win to lose," Darrius chuckled as he patted Nelson on his back and both men started laughing.

"I needed that laugh," Nelson said.

"No problem man," Darrius said with a big smile on his face.

"So did you ask his name?" Darrius asked.

"I was not ready for what she told me, so I just hung up," Nelson said.

"You should call her and at least let her explain," Darrius suggested.

"You right I will, but I did however send off for my

actual birth certificate. She seems to have lost it," Nelson said.

"Okay, I had to do the same thing. I couldn't find mine at all," Darrius said.

"How long did it take to come back?" Nelson asked.

"Hell, I will let you know when it comes!" Darrius said as he and Nelson burst out laughing.

"True. Besides, the holidays are coming up and I was going to go visit her then. Not sure if I want to now," Nelson said.

"Why is that?" Darrius asked.

"Because I will feel out of place. Like, do I really belong here?" Nelson asked.

"Well at the end of the day that is your family, that is who raised you," Darrius reminded him. Nelson just shook his head in agreement and didn't say anything, just looked as if he was deep in his thoughts.

"Didn't you say you had family around here?" Darrius asked.

"Yeah I do, but I don't know them that well. Only what my mother told me," Nelson answered.

"Feels weird don't it?" Darrius said.

"What?" Nelson said.

"Having to say mother after finding out this," Darrius said.

"Yeah it is. I was just thinking that?" Nelson said, giving Darrius an inquiring look.

"It's just a feeling I had," Darrius said.

"Okay, well you may not see me for a while after the holidays, I got a lot of other things I will be doing," Nelson said.

"I understand man, you got to do what you got to," Darrius said.

"Yeah and I think it will give me time to accept whatever it is my mother has to tell me," Nelson said.

"You're right," Darrius nodded.

"I do appreciate you coming out and talking with me," Nelson said.

"No problem. Anytime," Darrius said.

"I think I better head out before I get too drunk," Nelson chuckled.

"You okay to drive?" Darrius asked.

"Oh yeah, I got a driver," Nelson said as he swayed up from his seat. Darrius watched as Nelson walked out of the bar to his waiting driver. Darrius sat at the bar and looked over the menu even though he knew what he was going to order. He asked the bartender for a drink of water along with the juicy burger and fries. After Darrius got his meal and started to get good into it he got at least three bites before he started to feel his phone vibrate in his pocket.

His hands were too greasy to pick it up so he let the voicemail catch it. Darrius thought nothing of it until it started to ring again. He quickly cleaned his hands and pulled the phone from his pocket. It was Lizeth calling and he could see that he had a few missed calls and voicemails in his notification bar.

"Hello," Darrius answered with food still in his mouth.

"Darrius?" Lizeth said. Darrius could tell from her voice that something was wrong.

"Lizeth what is wrong?" Darrius asked.

"Your mother has been trying to reach you all day," Lizeth said with sadness in her voice.

"Is something wrong?" Darrius asked. The phone went silent for a few minutes. "Lizeth are you there?" Darrius asked with a million thoughts going through his head.

"Darrius you're father has taken ill they are not sure how long he has," Lizeth said as she started to cry.

Darrius' appetite quickly vanished. As he sat there for what seemed like forever he didn't even hear Lizeth as she was calling his name.

"Darrius answer me!" Lizeth yelled into the phone.

"I'm here. I am on my way home," Darrius said.

"No, tell me where you are and I will come to you," Lizeth said.

"Uhm, uhm, I'm at ah…" Darrius could hardly get his words out. "What do you mean ill? What is wrong with him?" Darrius asked.

"I will explain once I get to you," Lizeth said.

Not this, not now, Darrius thought to himself.

"Where are you?" Lizeth asked.

"I am at that sports bar downtown," Darrius said.

"I will be their shortly," Lizeth said and hung up the phone. Within thirty minutes, Lizeth was coming inside the doors. She walked over to him and sat next to him at the bar. She could tell that he had been drinking because he had the strong smell of alcohol on his breath.

"So I talked to my mother," Darrius said.

"Did she explain to you what was going on?" Lizeth asked.

"Yeah she did. She said my dad has cancer," Darrius said.

"I am so sorry," Lizeth said as she put her hand on top of

116

his.

"Why are you sorry? It's not like you gave him the cancer," Darrius shot back at her with anger.

"Darrius are you serious?" Lizeth said as she looked at him with confusion in her face.

"What? I am serious. I don't like when something goes wrong and the first thing somebody say is, I'm sorry," Darrius said, getting a little louder. People were starting to look in their direction.

"Darrius calm down," Lizeth said.

"No you calm down!" he yelled.

"Hey, do I need to have you escorted out?" The bartender said as he walked over.

"Please forgive him, he is dealing with a lot at the moment," Lizeth said to the bartender.

"I understand that may be the case, but if that continues he will need to leave," the bartender said as he walked off to serve other waiting customers.

"Darrius we need to go," Lizeth said gently as she reached for him to help him up.

"No you go, I'm good," Darrius said.

Lizeth could tell that he was drunk and out of control. She had never seen him this way before and she was starting to worry.

"You're so weak, you know that?" Darrius said as he looked at Lizeth with no emotion in his eyes.

"Darrius, you're drunk and hurting. Please let's go," Lizeth pleaded as she again tried to get him up, only to have her hand pushed away by Darrius.

"I am not drunk Lizeth, I only had two shots," Darrius lied. Lizeth looked over to the bartender. He was shaking his head in disagreement to what Darrius said.

"I don't know why I married you sometimes," Darrius said, his speech slurred. Lizeth was starting to get pissed, but she remained cool because she knew he was hurting and only trying to use displacement of his feelings on to her.

"I can get away with anything with you," Darrius said as he started to laugh.

"Darrius I need you to shut up," Lizeth said as she got up.

"No you shut the hell up!" Darrius screamed. "I am you're husband and you will listen to me," he snarled as he grabbed Lizeth arm.

"That's it you got to go," the bartender said.

"Fine I will!" Darrius yelled as he pulled Lizeth towards the door with him. Lizeth yanked her arm away from him and proceeded out the door without him. Darrius went after her. For someone who was clearly drunk he sure moved as if he was sober, Lizeth thought as she felt Darrius coming up behind her.

"What is wrong with you?" Darrius asked as he pushed Lizeth up against a parked car. Lizeth caught herself before she fell down.

"You bastard!" Lizeth hollered out as she turned around and slapped Darrius in his face. Darrius just stood and looked at Lizeth with his jaw tightening. She noticed that he had his fists balled up at his side. She was not sure what to expect at this point. Darrius just stood there for a moment before falling down on his knees with tears in his eyes.

"I'm going to lose him," Darrius said as he broke down in tears.

Chapter 7

"Damn that bitch almost caught me," Sam said out loud as she stood in the parking lot of Lizeth's job, watching her as she pulled off. To think that after watching Lizeth's every move for such a long time now, today the bitch decided to go off schedule. She don't know who she fucking with, Sam said to herself. Sam was just about to cut the brakes when she saw Lizeth coming out of the building, so she had to stop her initial plan and pretend as if she was coming to talk to her. After their little altercation Sam wished she had just gotten rid of Lizeth a long time ago. She thought if she put doubt in her head about her husband it would do the trick, but Lizeth was not going away that easily so it was time to up the ante.

Sam headed back to her apartment. She had a rather

lovely place. It was always immaculate and never a thing out of place. She was obsessed with neatness. She picked this apartment because it gave her the chance to be close to Darrius. The furniture was a rich, lush grey sofa with matching chairs on both sides of it, along with a designer rug that covered the polished floors. The walls were the purest of white, with not one picture on the wall. In the kitchen was the most stylish of appliances, all hi-tech in décor. The kitchen was in such order it looked as if it was never used. Her bedrooms matched the rest of the home with its immaculate cleanliness and style.

Sam walked over to a hidden door that sat to the far left in her second bedroom. The closet door was so easily missed you would not see it if you gave the room a quick glance over. She pulled the door open and walked in to reveal a nice sized walk-in closet space. One side of the wall was filled with pictures of Darrius, surrounded with hearts around him. On the shelf below the thousands of pictures sat plastered faces, each distinctive in style and texture of hair. Alongside them were cell phone contact cases with different colors. They all had names with them.

On the opposite wall were pictures of Lizeth, some with daggers in them and some with her face completely covered with black marker. From the looks of the pictures, you could tell someone had a lot of malice in their heart for her. There were pictures of her at work, in the shower at the gym, and even at home in bed with Darrius. It looked like a timeline of her day to day activities, as well as pictures that showed her undressed with special pictures blown up to show precise details of her body. Sam wanted to know her every move. From how she interacts to certain things as well as how her body looks to make sure she could mimic her to a tee. Sam looked down to a plaster mold she had been working on. It was her plaster mold replica of Lizeth's face. She had already gotten her day to day down, now she just had to finish her face to make it perfect for fitting.

Sam picked up the lifeless mold of a face and stared into its eyes. "Soon my biggest performance yet will get me the one I love," Sam said as she looked back at the thousands of pictures of Darrius on the wall. She sat down to her small vanity and opened her drawer to pull out a small contact case. She opened it up and began removing the green contacts out of her eyes to reveal her own natural eye color, which was honey brown in color. Sam then took off her lace front wig that was of a silky curly texture to reveal a more course type of hair.

Sam stared at herself for minutes before she removed the plaster mold of a face off. She was a medium built attractive woman. Her nose was a little pointy and her eyes were evenly spaced apart. She had high cheekbones and an overall ordinary face. The plaster face she had on was of her own, just without any flaws. Sam however, thought she was the ugliest of people. Whenever she looked into a mirror she would see an unattractive woman looking back at her.

"I can do this!" Sam shouted to her reflection in the mirror, as if her reflection was talking back. "You watch and see, he will be mine!" Sam said.

"Shut up!" Sam yelled to her reflection. She placed her hands on top of her head as if to silence the voices that only she could hear. "No! Shut up! Shut up! Shut up!" Sam screamed. Once she was satisfied with the voices now gone, she took a deep breath and applied the plaster mold replica of Lizeth's face onto hers. She then put in some contacts to make her honey brown eyes a dark brown eye color. She pulled out a lace front wing that was dark and silky in texture to match that of Lizeth's hair.

She applied her finishing touches and once she was complete, there in the mirror looking back at her was Lizeth and no longer Sam. Sam had become so comfortable with

Lizeth that she could even mimic her voice to where no one would know the difference. Sam got undressed and applied a coat of grease-like make up to the front part of her body to a much darker completion. She was pleased with the look so far. Sam then had a machine set to spray her bare body on her backside. After the machine was done spraying, Sam looked herself over. She was happy with her results. I am Sam no more, call me Lizeth, Sam said to herself as looked in the mirror.

Sam thought it was time to see if she could get away with being Lizeth so she planned on going out once Lizeth and Darrius left for the holidays. According to their schedule they were set to leave in a few days. Sam put on an outfit that matched one of Lizeth's. She walked out of her hidden room and out of her apartment. She went to the car garage and instead of driving her own car, she chose to drive her 2015 Audi, which was the same as Lizeth's car, but Sam had tinted windows on hers that were a little darker then Lizeth's. Sam headed out to go see if she could fool Darrius.

"What better way to pull this off, then to fool the one you love," Sam laughed aloud as she started the car and headed out.

*****

Darrius laid back on the bed contemplating on all that has happened to him over the last few days. His father was sick and may soon be dying. He felt as if life as he knew it was just becoming a big mess. Darrius and Lizeth planned to head out to his parents' for the holidays. However, Lizeth had to take care of some things so she would not be leaving out with him. Darrius got up from the bed and went to his closet to retrieve his suitcase and clothes to take with him. His cell phone started to ring, he went to answer it and he notice that it was Lizeth calling.

"Hello," Darrius answered.

"How are you feeling?" Lizeth asked.

"I am ok for the most part," Darrius answered.

"Well it looks like I will be able to leave out with you," Lizeth said.

"That's great," Darrius said.

"Yeah, but I may have to come back early," Lizeth said.

"It's always something," Darrius said, shaking his head.

"It's my job," Lizeth said.

"Yeah, anyway I got to pack," Darrius said and hung up the phone. Darrius was getting a little frustrated that Lizeth had been putting her job ahead of him lately and it was becoming an issue for him. He never wanted her to work. He knew it would cause problems.

Sam made her way up the steps to where Darrius was. She could hear him on the phone as she snuck inside of the house. She stood outside the room just admiring him for a moment before walking into the room. Darrius turned around and gave her a glance then went back to his packing.

"Are you upset?" Sam asked in her best Lizeth voice.

"I thought me hanging up would have been a clear indication that I am," Darrius said with attitude.

So far so good, Sam thought to herself. He thinks I am her. "What can I do to make it right?" Sam asked.

"Really, you should already know the answer to that," Darrius said as he stopped packing and turned around to face her.

"You look different, you wore that to work?" Darrius asked as he looked her up and down.

"Yes I did," Sam said as she glanced down at her outfit. "So what can I do to make it better?" Sam asked, referring to the question she asked earlier.

"You can quit your job," Darrius stated.

"If that will make you happy I will do that and whatever

else," Sam said. Darrius gave her a look of shock and then he smiled.

"Are you serious?" he asked as he walked over to her and stared at her for a second, then giving her a long passionate kiss. Sam was starting to feel weak in her knees. She wanted him right there and now, but she knew that Lizeth would be home shortly. Sam pulled back from his grip.

"What's wrong?" Darrius asked.

"Nothing," Sam said. "I just need to go put something up that I brought in down stairs."

"Now?" he said.

"Yes, it will be just a second," Sam said.

"Okay, hurry back," Darrius said as he smacked her on her butt. Sam's heart was beating a mile a minute. She knew she had to hurry because the tracker in her pocket was vibrating rather fast, indicating to her that Lizeth was nearby. She installed the tracker on her car when she came to visit her one afternoon. What she did not need was her plan to fall apart this soon.

Sam made her way down the stairs just as Lizeth was turning the key. Sam ran into the dining room as Lizeth was walking inside with bags in her hand.

"Darrius can you come help me?" Lizeth called out. Darrius came down the steps with a smile on his face that quickly faded when he noticed all the bags.

"I thought you said you had to put something up? I didn't know you had to get it out of the car," Darrius said.

"What are you talking about?" Lizeth asked.

"You just told me you had to put something up," Darrius said.

"Darrius I just got here, I have not spoken to you since you hung up on me," Lizeth said, shaking her head. They both walked towards the kitchen and Sam could hear them talking.

She wanted to wait around to listen in on the up and coming argument that she knew was coming. Darrius thinks Lizeth told him that she would quit her job. Oh boy will that be a fight! Sam thought as she slipped out of the house.

"When did you change your clothes?" Darrius asked as he and Lizeth sat at the island in the kitchen to eat their dinner.

"I didn't, I had this on all day," Lizeth said, giving him a confused look. "Are you ok?"

"I'm fine, are you?" Darrius asked, giving Lizeth the same confusing look. "Whatever. You did not just have that on a few minutes ago," he said, shaking his head.

"A few--. Wait, what? I just walked in the door!" Lizeth said.

"So when are you packing up?" Darrius asked.

"After dinner," Lizeth said.

"I thank you for making that decision. With everything that is going on I really appreciate it," Darrius said.

Lizeth was about to ask him what he was talking about when the house phone started to ring and he got up to answer it. Darrius came back and said it was the hotel confirming their reservations.

*****

Sam watched as they pulled out of the garage and headed to the highway. She had been staking out their home all morning to make sure they both left. Sam intended to go to Lizeth's job as her and ask for some time off so that she could have enough time to get in the role of Lizeth, as well as get rid of her before anyone noticed anything strange. Now that Darrius wanted her to quit, it would be easy to become his housewife, something he wanted anyway. Sam felt it was time to remove Lizeth so that she could have Darrius to herself and not have to take on the role of the other woman any longer.

Sam knew that Darrius would not leave Lizeth, as he told her on many occasions. She pretended to be each and every woman that he slept with, at least that is how it happened in her dreams. Sam began to have flashbacks of each role she played out, and each time she was in different character with Darrius. I am done being them. They can't keep him, only she can," Sam thought to herself as she stared straight ahead at the house. Sam started the car and headed towards Lizeth's job.

****

"Mrs. Jackson, I thought you left for out of town for a few days?" Lizeth's secretary said as Sam came through the door.

"Well I came in to handle some business."

"Is there something I can help you with?" she asked.

"Yes I need to talk to the partners."

"Mrs. Jackson is something wrong?" she asked with a nervous voice. Sam could see that she was nervous.

"It is important, but it has nothing to do with you."

She exhaled a sign of relief and immediately got on the phone to set up a meeting. Sam walked into Lizeth's office and looked around. Lizeth was always neat and her office looked beautiful. She had a large cherry wood desk with matching soft leather chairs, beautiful paintings on the wall and two large bookshelves filled with the latest law books. There was a beautiful view of the city and the lighting in the office was set perfectly.

There on the desk was a picture of Lizeth and Darrius, one Sam had never seen before. She went over to it and picked it. Something inside of her filled with rage and she threw the photo across the room. It shattered once it made contact with the bookcase. Sam picked up the broken frame and took the picture out. She stared into Darrius eyes and kissed the picture as if it were she he were looking at. She then looked at Lizeth and tore the picture in half. She placed the half with Darrius in her pocket and the other half in the trash bin. She turned around and saw that the sectary had been standing there watching her with a look of shock on her face.

"Uhm, I knocked on the door. Just wanted to let you know the partners said they would see you now," she said as she backed out of the office. Sam was about to explain what

131

she saw to her but at this point, she no longer cared. She went into the conference room to explain to the partners that she would be leaving the firm indefinitely. They tried to convince her to stay but it was no use, she had made up her mind. She walked out of the conference room with a smile on her face. The secretary that worked for Lizeth thought her behavior today was just off, being that she had just spoken with her before she came in. Sam walked out of the building with great joy, she even told the partners not to contact her. She got in her car and drove back towards Lizeth and Darrius' home. Now all she had to do was sit and wait for the next part of her plan to unfold.

As Darrius pulled up into his parents' estate his nerves were starting to get the best of him. He didn't know if he could handle seeing his father, a man so strong and healthy, weak and dying. Darrius turned the car off and sat in the car staring at the house, the same house he grew up in with many happy memories. Lizeth sat with him and put her hand on his.

"Are you okay?" she asked.

"Yeah, I just need a minute."

"Okay." They sat in the car in silence for a good ten minutes before the front door opened and his mother came out.

Darrius' mother was beautiful. She had such beautiful caramel skin and long grey hair. You could tell from her features that she was a knock out in her earlier days. She was short and nicely shaped for a woman of her age. The only thing that looked as if it aged was her hair, but even it was neatly done. She was about 5'6, compared to Darrius' father who stood at 6'3. All the men in the family were tall. Lizeth got out to greet her. She always wore a welcoming smile.

"Lizeth, it's so good to see you," she smiled.

"It's great to see you as well ma," Lizeth said as she gave her a big hug.

"Yes, just wish it was not this type of visit," she said.

"You're right, but I am glad we are here," Lizeth said. Darrius got out of the car and came around and hugged his mother.

"Darrius, look at you!" she said with a big smile.

"Hi mama, I missed you so much," he said.

"I know, that's why you call me so much," she joked.

"Ma, come on now, you know I be busy."

"Yeah that's what your brothers say," she laughed.

"Are they coming down?" Lizeth asked.

"No they got tied up. Besides, I think this is more for

Darrius than them," she answered.

"What do you mean?" Darrius asked.

"Let's get your things in the house and I will explain everything to you, okay?" she said as she ushered Lizeth into the house.

Chapter 8

Darrius forgot to let his mother know that he and Lizeth had agreed on staying at a hotel, but he planned to tell her once he got around to it. With so much going on, Darrius was forgetting many things. Darrius could hear his mom and Lizeth in the kitchen talking. He instead walked up the steps to his old bedroom. He walked in and to his dismay it was no longer his bedroom, but an office. Why did they need another office in this big house? he wondered. Darrius decided to leave his old bedroom and go in search of his father.

Darrius walked through the house until he was standing directly in front of his parents' bedroom door. He could remember all the times when he was young coming into their bedroom and spending time with his dad talking and discussing everything. Darrius felt himself tearing up, but he quickly composed himself. To think, this could be the last time that he walked into this room and saw his father. That hurt him deeply. Darrius knocked on the door. He could hear the TV from inside the room. His dad enjoyed game shows and it sounded as if Wheel of Fortune was on.

"Come in," a voice from inside the room said. Darrius was not sure who that voice was but he was sure it was not his dad's. When he opened the door he could feel the warmness of the room as he walked in. It was much warmer than the rest of the house. A middle-aged woman walked up to him. She looked to be a nurse.

"Hi, my name is Mattie," she introduced herself as she extended her hand to him.

"Hi, how are you? I am Darrius," he replied.

"Yes I know, your father goes on about you all the time," she said with a smile.

"How is he doing?" he asked.

"Well, he is resting at the moment, he should be awake in a few hours," she told him.

"Okay, well I will come back then," Darrius said as he turned and walked out of the room.

Darrius found Lizeth and his mother in the small living room of the house. They were looking over photo albums of Darrius as a child. It seemed to be a tradition or something with his mother. She would show pictures each time they came to visit and with each visit a new photo would appear, one that Darrius couldn't remember ever taking.

"Showing old photos again," Darrius said as he joined them in the living room.

"I will show them as much as I like," his mother said. "Did you see your dad?" she asked.

"No not yet, he was sleeping," Darrius said.

"Yeah he does that a lot," she said with hurt in her eyes.

"Mom it's going to be okay," Darrius insisted.

"I know, but that does not stop the hurt," she said softly.

"Mom, why didn't you tell me that he was this bad off?" Darrius asked.

"He asked me not to. You know how your father is. When he wants you to know he will tell you."

"Well, I got a visit from Travis," Darrius said.

"I am aware of it, he called," she said.

"So did he mention our conversation?" Darrius asked. His mother nodded her head and just looked as if the weight of the world was on her shoulders. Lizeth could see that maybe they were having some kind of coded conversation without saying much.

"Darrius what's going on?" Lizeth asked. The room went silent for a few seconds.

"That's what I'm trying to find out," he said. They both faced his mother who was standing in pure silence.

"Look, you two just got here, can we enjoy each other's company before we discuss all that needs to be discussed?" she finally answered.

What is with the prolonging of it? Darrius wondered to himself. Maybe there was some truth to what Travis said. Darrius could sense how odd his mother was behaving.

"Fine we can wait, but I want answers today," Darrius told his mother.

Lizeth could feel some light tension between the two of them. However, she decided to leave it alone and not say anything. Her cell phone has been buzzing with notifications of messages and missed calls from her secretary. A few of the calls came from other employees at the firm as well. She was not sure why everyone was reaching out to her, they knew she was out of town. Besides, what was going on here was more important than what the office needed. She decided she would check the messages later. Her only concern was her husband. Despite everything, he needed her.

Darrius informed his mom that he and Lizeth would be staying at a hotel instead of at the estate with them. She understood and without any protest, said no more of it. Darrius felt like that was not like his mother so he could not wait any longer.

"Mom are you okay?" he asked. The expression on her face told a story she was not telling.

"Just don't think of me differently," she said.

"Why? What is going on, why I would think less of you?"

"Not now Darrius. Let us just get ready for dinner, maybe your father will join us.".

"Fine," he said. Darrius was getting aggravated with all the silence. He wanted to know if what Travis said was true.

Darrius was silent at dinner. His father's nurse came down to inform everyone that his father decided to have his dinner upstairs, he was too tired to come down. However, he wanted to talk with Darrius afterwards. Darrius finished up his meal rather quickly and as he headed up the stairs his mother stopped him in the hall.

"Darrius please understand," was all she said as she walked back towards the kitchen.

Darrius made his way back to his parents' room and the door was ajar since he was expected. The same warmth he felt earlier brushed across his face again as he entered the room. The nurse Mattie was sitting in a chair reading a book next to the bed. Darrius walked up and around the big king-sized bed to the side his father was laying on. He looked at his father and almost did not recognize him. His once full head of dark hair was no more. His body frame that held his broad shoulders were small and shrunken. He looked more of a fragile version of his once strong self. His father's eyes remained dark and full of life despite his outer appearance. Darrius could not take the look much longer and he was about to walk away until his father spoke.

"Don't run from me," he said as if he could read his son's very thoughts.

"Dad I can't stand to see you like this," Darrius said.

"Would you prefer me in a casket and not moving?" his father asked. He still had his sense of humor as well as his deep voice. His father sat up in the bed as much as he could. Darrius offered to help him get more comfortable but he refused it.

"It's good to see you son," his father said.

"It's good to see you to dad."

140

"I know you have many questions son."

Darrius nodded in agreement. "I do."

"I will try an answer them, but what I can't answer your mother will," his father said.

"I understand," Darrius nodded. His father went on to tell him how he met his mother and that when he saw her he knew she was the one for him.

"When I first met your mother she was all I wanted. She was beautiful and I loved her instantly. I couldn't see myself without her so when the opportunity presented itself I asked her to marry me. She was so sweet and naïve," he said, reminiscing on the good days. Darrius gave his father an expression to signify that he did not like that comment. "I see you have my temper," his father chuckled, noticing his expression. "Just calm down, and allow me to explain. The reason I said she was naïve was because she trusted me. She loved me so much that she didn't notice how awful I really was. I cheated on your mother a lot. I would leave for long periods of times and she thought it was work. No matter how much I loved her I still couldn't be faithful. My pride got the best of me. As long as I took care of home I felt I should be able to do as I pleased," his father said.

He again began to cough a lot harder this time. The

nurse was about to come to him but he told her he was okay. Darrius started to have flashes of his own flaws and the conversation he had with his bother came to mind.

"I couldn't understand why I did what I did. It went on for so long, only because no matter what I did I could always come home to your mother. She would have me with open arms no matter what. I stopped feeling bad about it, I knew she had to know," his father went on, but all Darrius could see in his mind was his mother crying and hurt. Then he began seeing Lizeth crying and hurt and he could feel the anger boiling in him. He was not sure if he was mad at his father or at himself for being just like him. His father went on to tell him about how he was verbally abusive to his mother as well. He told him that he had so many women that he could not keep count. Darrius was enraged.

"Darrius are you listening to me?" he asked. Darrius did not speak he was too afraid of what might come out.

"Why are you telling me this?" he asked his father.

"Because I wanted you to know that what you're going through is not just you," his father said knowingly. Darrius looked at his father shocked that he too knew about his situation. "Yes I know about all that you're going through," his father spoke with concern.

"My situation has nothing to do with what you did to mom," Darrius said with arrogance.

"You're stubborn like your mother," his father said.

"Don't you dare talk about my momma," Darrius said and got up from the bed. He did not want to hear anymore.

"Sit down," his father said loudly. The nurse looked up but remained silent and continued to read her book.

"Like hell," Darrius muttered. Despite his father being weak and ill he still had his smarts and wits about him. Darrius was indeed mad but he knew better than to cross his dad or disrespect him, which he would not do. Darrius remained standing.

"You have every reason to be upset," his father said.

"How could you be so damn grimey?" Darrius shouted.

"How can you?" his father shot back. "I did it the same way you do it, with a straight damn face," his father said. Darrius felt that blow. It hurt because it was true.

"Boy you heard of generational curses?" his father asked. Darrius nodded his head. He wasn't the most active churchgoer but he did remember a sermon about it.

"You feel that's what's going on here?" he asked.

"I do," his father nodded.

"Why is it when people do wrong they want to go all

143

churchy?" Darrius said, shaking his head in disbelief.

"Why would you say something so simple?" his father asked.

"It's the truth! You're trying to say it's a curse now, that what you did was not you," Darrius said.

"No that is not what I'm saying. I'm trying to educate you on something," his father said. "I know I was wrong, I have made my peace with what I did. What about you?" his father asked.

"Whatever," Darrius mumbled. "My wife and my situation don't have a thing to do with this," Darrius said.

"Yes it does. I told your mother my wrongs years before I found out I was sick. She was the only one to stand by my side once I got ill. The other women did not care," his father told him.

"So what is it you want from me?" Darrius asked.

"Nothing. I can't ask for your forgiveness because it's too soon, but that's on you. When you were younger you started to act out because of the way you saw me treat your mother."

"I don't remember you mistreating mom," Darrius said.

"That's because of that place we sent you to," his father said. Darrius gave his father a puzzled look.

"What place?"

His father started to cough and the nurse walked over to check him out. Darrius moved to give her room.

"You will need to rest soon," Mattie said.

"I was a different man back then. Not only was I cheating, but I was verbally abusive to you mother. You were so close to me but then you started acting out, blaming your mother for me not being home. Your temper was out of control. Your mother couldn't deal with it, so we got you professional help," he explained.

Darrius was in shock. How could they keep so much from him for so long? His father continued to tell him about a local place he was sent to first. They could not help him so he was sent to a place in Arizona. The therapist and team there did so well with him that when he came back he was like a new person. His father said the family decided never to speak of his past or having to go away again.

Darrius just stared off into space. He was at a loss for words. So many things were going through his head he was not sure if he was coming or going.

"I don't know if I know who I am now," Darrius said.

"I know it's a lot, but I wanted to tell you before I---,"

Darrius looked at his father, it was as if he was looking

at a stranger. "You're clearly not the man I thought you were. I think it will be best if I leave now," Darrius said, turning to leave. He was angry, pissed and hurt. All at the same time.

"I understand," his father said quietly. Darrius walked out of the room and stood in the hall for a moment. He had to get his thoughts together. Darrius walked back into the kitchen and was instantly angry once he saw his mother.

"How could you stay with him?" he asked her. His mother turned around once she heard his voice and looked at him. "Were you desperate or was it the money?"

"How dare you, speak to me like that!" his mother said.

"How dare you lie to me?" he asked.

"I don't owe you any explanations," she said defiantly.

"Like hell! You're no different than him," Darrius spat. Lizeth looked at them both. She was shocked to hear how disrespectful Darrius was being. His mother and her were just cleaning and not really talking about much.

Lizeth had asked her what was going on just before Darrius came into the kitchen, but she said she would have to ask Darrius so Lizeth left it alone. Darrius' mother put down her dishtowel, walked over to Darrius and slapped him.

"You will not disrespect me in my house," she said as she walked out of the kitchen. Lizeth walked over to Darrius, but before she could reach him he had already turned away. He followed his mother. She sat down on the couch and he could see the hurt in her eyes. Darrius no longer felt any sympathy for her as he once did. Just like his father, his mother was looking unfamiliar as well.

"I need answers," Darrius demanded.

"You will get them, but tell me how can you be mad that I stayed by your father's side, when you are doing the same to your wife?" she asked, staring down at the floor. Darrius could see the tears in her eyes but they did not faze him.

"My situation has nothing to do with this," Darrius said.

"I had to forgive your father and I did. I didn't do it for him, I did it for me. And your situation does have to do with this, it's the same. Besides that, I have much to tell you," she said.

"What now?" he asked. She began to tell him about how she was hurt by what his father did to her and that she had to forgive him only because it was best for her. She also told him that she wanted to get even with his father and really hurt him, so she gave up one of her children only to tell his father that he died.

"You gave up a child?" Darrius asked.

"I did, you had a bother," she admitted.

147

"How could that hurt him?" Darrius asked.

"No matter what your father did, he loved all of you. So my best revenge would be to tell him I lost your brother. In the end it hurt me instead, so when you father came home one day I told him the truth. He demanded to know but I would never tell him where your brother was,"

Darrius was shocked and stunned that the two people he thought he knew were complete strangers.

"I have a hoe for a father and a liar for a mother!" Darrius shouted.

"You will not talk to me that way!" she yelled.

"I don't understand how you did not know your husband was cheating on you," Darrius said.

"I did know. We women always know, but it was my choice to stay," she said.

"You know what? I don't care anymore. Why would you give my brother up?" Darrius demanded.

"I could not handle five boys on my own and your father was barley around."

Darrius was just tired. Today was a long day. He was pissed and he needed air. His mother was still talking. She said that it was a bad choice she made and how she thought about going back for her child but felt it would be best if he stayed where he was. Darrius was spent, he wanted to get far away from his parents as soon as possible. Who are these people? he thought. Darrius was so angry, more at his mother for being so selfish. Lizeth walked into the den to join them and again it was silent, but the looks on their faces told an untold story.

"What's going on?" she asked.

"Nothing, we will talk later. I need a few minutes with her," Darrius said, no longer feeling the need to call her mom. Lizeth stood and again walked away clueless.

"Why did you send me away, was I a burden too? " Darrius asked. She walked over to comfort him but he pulled back.

"Darrius you were not a burden, I just wanted to get you help," she said with sorrow in her eyes. "Please don't hate me," she said.

"I don't hate you, I just don't know you," he said.

"Darrius I need to tell you one more thing," she said. Darrius looked at his mother and he could see just how bad whatever it was, was wearing down on her. She grabbed her chest, sat down and stared at the floor. The tears were coming down her face a lot more now.

"Darrius, the brother I gave away, he was your twin."

Darrius' mind went blank, he could no longer hear. He was trying to wrap his mind around at what she just said. Did she just say that to me?

"What did you just say?" Darrius asked. She was just standing there. Darrius could see her lips moving but could not hear a sound, he could read her lips and she did say what he thought she said. "My twin?" Darrius went from zero to one hundred very quick. "What the fuck!" he yelled.

Darrius was beyond furious. He yelled for Lizeth to come on so they could leave. His mother tried to talk to him and reach out for him, but he would not hear it. Lizeth came to join him outside. She turned to hug his mother, but Darrius was rushing her to come on. Darrius sped off from his parents' house. The drive was short because of his speeding. Lizeth was shocked that he was not pulled over by the police. Darrius filled Lizeth in on what his parents told him, minus what they said about him cheating as well.

Once they checked into their room Darrius took all of his frustration out on Lizeth in the bed. He fucked her as if he never fucked her before. He could tell she was not use to him being so rough as she was pleading for him to stop, but he continued until he reached his satisfaction. Once Lizeth passed out Darrius could not find sleep. He kept tossing and turning, hearing his parent's voices repeatedly. Darrius' mother called the room a few times but he refused to speak to her. Darrius was upset that Lizeth gave her the room number and told her to call front desk to stop all the calls coming into the room, but she refused.

Darrius got up from the bed and stood on the balcony outside of the room. He felt like he could stay there in the cool breeze air just enjoying this brief moment forever. However, he knew it was not the case. He had to go back into the room to face reality. He had to face his parents to get the answers and take care of all that's been going on lately. Lizeth sat up in the bed and just stared at her husband as he paced back and forth on the balcony. She could not imagine all the things going through his head right now. All the secrets his family held from him. Maybe they just held it out of love, she thought to herself.

It was at that moment she felt she should just tell him that she knew about the other women and all his issues he was having at work. However, she changed her mind seeing that he was dealing with enough now. Lizeth decided to get out of bed and check on some of her missed emails. She looked over to the clock and saw that it was too late to return her secretary's call so she just used the free WIFI and went through her emails. She noticed that she had many emails most from co-workers and some from the partners and a few from clients. Strange, she thought so she opened one.

It was the basic office letterhead along with appreciation for her time and work, but as she continued to read the words, "Sorry to see you go" caught her attention. "Go?" she said to herself. Lizeth kept on reading and it said she quit today. Lizeth went through the other emails and noticed that they all pretty much said the same thing. What the hell is going on? Lizeth wondered. She needed to talk to her secretary and now. She reached for her phone to dial her secretary but her secretary was already calling her.

"What is going on?" Lizeth asked without saying hello to her.

"I don't know! You came into the office and quit," she said.

"How? But I'm here," Lizeth said.

"That's what's strange," her secretary said.

"What do you mean?" Lizeth asked. The secretary began telling her about how she acted when she came into the office and how she demanded to speak with the partners. She told her that when she went into her office she saw her tear up a picture of herself and Darrius, only to throw her picture in the trash and keep Darrius' picture in her pocket.

"I did not do any of that!" Lizeth said.

"Mrs. Jackson I don't know what to say," her secretary said.

"Trust I will be back there tomorrow to see what is going on," Lizeth said.

They hung up with nothing more to say. Darrius came into the room.

"What's going on?" he asked. Lizeth was upset and confused about what just happened.

"Apparently I went into the job and quit, according to my secretary and the emails I just read," she explained.

"Ok, so," Darrius said nonchalantly. Lizeth had to raise an eyebrow on that comment.

"So, what you mean by so?" she asked assertively.

"Exactly what I said. Shit, you said you was quitting anyway," he reminded her.

"I never said that," she denied.

"That's what the hell you told me before we left to come up here,"

Chapter 9

"Darrius have you lost your damn mind? How can I go in the office and quit when I am here with you?

"Look, I don't have time for your mind games woman, I got my own shit to worry about!" he yelled. Darrius wished he could take that last sentence back but it was too late.

"Mind games, Mind games? I am not paying mind games with anyone!" Lizeth screamed back. Lizeth went over to the closet to retrieve her things. She was fed up with his attitude and she just needed to get away from him before she snapped.

"Where are you going?" Darrius asked.

"Leaving!" she answered.

Darrius shook his head with disbelief. "I don't have time

for this shit," he grumbled as he turned to walk back out to the balcony. Lizeth, now fully dressed, stopped packing her things. Darrius must have hit a nerve because now she was pissed to the point of no return.

"Fuck you mean you don't have time for this shit?" she yelled. Darrius turned to face her. "Let me tell you what I don't have time for! A cheating, two timing, no good, trifling husband. I don't have time for secrets and bullshit. I don't have time for your lies and your fucked up attitude. Just know I don't owe you shit. Yes I know about all the bullshit you been doing, but I was still here by your side, yet you give me nothing but bullshit!" Lizeth was so mad she didn't realize how loud she was getting. "I know everything!" she screamed. Darrius tried to speak but Lizeth cut him off.

"No you listen. I had to go behind you to find out what you would not tell me. That's fucked up," Lizeth said.

Lizeth was determined not to shed one single tear and as hard as it was she did just that. Darrius, with a look of guilt on his face tried to walk over to her. Lizeth backed away from him. "Don't touch me, I don't want your damn sympathy," she said maliciously.

Lizeth finished packing her things. She was so mad she just wanted to get away. She has never got that mad at anyone as long as she could remember. "I'm going back home to tend to my business, I suggest you stay here and handle your business," Lizeth said as she grabbed her things and stormed out of the door.

Darrius was lost for words. What could he say? The truth was out and the bad part is Lizeth knew everything. The fucked up part about it is that she didn't hear it from me, Darrius thought to himself. Everything his brother, mother and father said came at him like a flood. He was sure he lost her now. He was so lost in his own world that he never considered telling his wife about everything and now it may be too late.

*****

Lizeth arrived back to her office around 10:30. The drive was just a few hours. She considered going home before coming to the office so that she could drive back, but she quickly decided against it since she had already accumulated a fee. She figured she might as well ride all the way to her office. Even though it was a mini holiday, her office was still open. As a lawyer, you do not have too many days off. Darrius had been calling and texting her nonstop since she left. She ignored all his calls and text messages. For once, Lizeth was just thinking of herself. She was being selfish and at this point she no longer cared, she felt she was in the right to be just that. Yes, Darrius had a lot going on but so did she, and as of right now they needed this time apart.

*****

Walking the hotel floor was becoming tiresome for Darrius. He repeatedly called and texted Lizeth and each time he called it went straight to voicemail. He was about to follow her but he knew she was still upset and he needed to at least have some space between them before he tried to explain his self. Thinking about it, what could he say to soften the hurt? Darrius decided to go back to his parents' house to try to hear them out. He was on his way out of the house when his cell phone rang. He thought it was Lizeth calling ready to talk, so he answered it, not recognizing the number.

"Lizeth?" Darrius answered hopefully.

"Ah, no man, it's me, Nelson."

"Oh hey man, how you doing?" Darrius said, a little embarrassed.

"Good, is everything okay?" Nelson asked compassionately.

"No, Lizeth found out about everything."

"Wow really, sorry to hear that man."

"Yeah we had a big fight and she left. Now she's not returning my calls," Darrius said.

"Damn. Well I was calling to tell you I found out something," Nelson said.

"Okay, what is it?" Darrius asked. Nelson went on to tell Darrius that he found out that he was in an institution for troubled teens for a few months in his younger days. While he was there another teen patient had become obsessed with him.

Darrius told Nelson what his parents told him, and that he couldn't recall anything about being there.

"Do you remember a girl by the name of Samantha Carr?" Nelson asked him.

"No, I can't recall anyone by that name," Darrius said, trying to figure out if he knew anyone by that name.

"Well she was the teen at the institution that became obsessed with you to the point that they felt it would be best if you were moved to another location, far from her," Nelson explained.

Darrius was trying to search in his mind to see if he could recall anything but he couldn't. Nelson told him that Samantha was very toxic and dangerous. She was a master manipulator who suffered from many personality disorders that caused her to believe she is people she is not.

He also told him that her obsession could become deadly, and if she felt someone was in her way she would even go as far as killing. Darrius was a little intimidated but not concerned until Nelson informed him that she may have killed a few people and that she had not been heard from in years. She was considered extremely dangerous and had escaped from the institution. Darrius became nervous.

"Why am I just hearing of this?" Darrius asked.

"Well according to my sources, they figured she was no real threat to you, being it has been years," Nelson said.

Darrius was shocked and hated that he could not remember any of it. He told Nelson that he would get the missing information from his parents. Nelson agreed and told him that he would send over an updated picture of the girl to jog his memory. They hung up and Darrius left out to his parents' house to get the missing pieces to the puzzle.

*****

Lizeth made it up to her floor and was stopped by an unfamiliar woman who was sitting at her secretary's desk.

"How can I help you?" she asked Lizeth.

Lizeth looked at the woman and could see that she was new. "Where is the young lady whose desk this is?"

"Oh, she walked away for a moment," the young lady answered.

"Okay."

"I am just sitting here until she comes back, I just started today," she said.

"I need to speak with Mr. James," Lizeth said.

"Mr. James is a very busy man and I doubt he is here," she said.

"I am Lizeth Jackson and I am sure he will see me," Lizeth said. The young woman's eyes went big.

"Oh my God, I just love you! You're an amazing attorney," she complimented.

"Thank you. Can you please find out if he is here?" Lizeth asked.

"Yes I will," she nodded as she got on the phone to find out where he was. As Lizeth waited, her secretary came from down the hall and gave her a big hug.

"Mrs. Jackson, you're back!"

"Yes, so we need to handle this problem," Lizeth said.

"Yes indeed. Would you like to go into your office? They have not touched it," she said.

"Sure."

Both women walked to Lizeth's office. The other secretary walked in to let them know that Mr. James would be coming down to talk to her.

"How can you fix this?" her secretary asked.

"Easy, I have something that whoever it was didn't know I had in my office," Lizeth said. Her secretary gave her a look of confusion.

"What do you mean?" she asked.

"You will see," Lizeth said. They waited in her office until Mr. James arrived, along with the other two partners in tow.

"Mrs. Jackson, have you changed your mind?" he asked her as he walked into the office.

"I never said I was leaving," Lizeth said.

"How is that possible? We all saw you and heard you loud and clear," said one of the partners standing beside Mr. James.

"Right," Mr. James nodded, agreeing with the man

standing next to him. Lizeth went on to tell them how it was impossible that she was in the office when she was out of town with her husband. Then she explained to them that she had been on the phone with her secretary at the same time she supposedly walked in and quit. They said she could have come in right after the phone call.

Lizeth gave them proof. She showed them a video of her office and informed them that she had the cameras installed for recording of meetings with clients in the office and over the phone.

"I forgot to turn the camera off when I left and I'm glad I didn't," Lizeth said.

She played the video and fast forwarded it for the day she left. They could see she was in a meeting with a client doing the normal business. Then she fast-forwarded it to the day she was supposed to have come into the office when she was clearly out of town. They watched as she came into the office and looked around as if the office was new to her. Then she threw a picture from her desk to the ground. They watched her pick up the picture and rip it in half, then kiss her husband and throw the picture of herself in the trash. Lizeth looked on in horror and shock as the woman on the screen looked to be her, but she was certain that she did not do that. The video stopped when her secretary stood in the doorway and watched in horror at her boss' display. Lizeth looked around at everyone and their looks still seemed as if they were not convinced.

"As it may seem, Mrs. Jackson that is you on the video," Mr. James said.

"That is not me!" Lizeth protested.

"Mrs. Jackson I don't understand the issue, I see you clearly on the tape here," Mr. James said.

"But sir that is not me! Why would I behave like that?"

"I am not sure, maybe the work load is too much," Mr. James shrugged.

"Since when was work ever an issue for me?" Lizeth said coldly.

"I don't know, Mrs. Jackson," Mr. James said as he and the gentlemen began to walk towards the door.

"Mr. James, think about this, I have been with this firm for a while. Why would I just up and quit, knowing I missed work?" Lizeth said.

"Either way, you decided to leave us," Mr. James answered.

"However, I am here now telling you that I did not quit and that I did not come into the office on that day. I will prove it," Lizeth said.

"How can you prove it? The video spoke volumes," Mr. James asked.

"Look at the time on the video," Lizeth said as she pointed to the tape where she had it paused.

"Okay, it says that you were here at 11:15 p.m." one of the men in suits said. Lizeth went into her purse, and pulled out her cell phone and opened her call log to show that at exactly 11:15 she was just getting off the phone with the office talking to her secretary. Then she logged into her computer to show the logs on the phone system that the office records as well.

After showing all this to everyone the room went quiet for a while. Everyone was stunned and at a loss for words.

"I don't have a twin," Lizeth said, breaking the silence.

"I am not sure what is going on, but I'm glad that it was not you," Mr. James said.

"Yes sir," Lizeth said.

"Well if someone would go through that much trouble to be you, there is no telling what else they would do. Be careful, you may need to call the authorities," Mr. James advised.

"I will," Lizeth said.

"I look forward to seeing you back to work after your vacation," Mr. James said as he and the gentlemen in suits walked out of the office.

*****

After talking with his parents and trying to keep an open mind, Darrius felt a little bit better. He did not want to be at war with his father since he was seriously ill and he allowed his mother to explain in detail about everything. They told him that when he went to get help the first time, the reason he had to leave that place was because a girl named Samantha became obsessed with him and they felt it was dangerous for him and it would stop his treatment if he remained there. Therefore, they sent him to Arizona, far away from her. Then they found out that around the time he left she went missing. Darrius was talking to his parents when his phone rang. It was Nelson.

"What's up man?" Darrius answered.

"Hey, I was just calling you to let you know that I should be getting the picture soon, but I am on my way to see my sick dad," Nelson said.

"Oh, I forgot about that. I hope that all goes well, I am

visiting my father as well," Darrius said.

"Oh okay. Well I got to go, I'm driving. I should be at my dad house in a minute," Nelson said.

"Okay, well send the picture when you can," Darrius said as they hung up. It must have been five minutes later when Nelson sent Darrius a picture of Samantha Carr. Darrius almost feel to his knees. This can't be right.

Darrius told his parents he had to leave. He rushed out of their house and dialed up Nelson. Nelson answered on the first ring.

"You got the picture?" Nelson asked.

"That can't be right. The woman you sent me a picture of is an intern that use to be shadow me at my job."

"What?" Nelson said.

"Yeah, I have known her for a few months and her name is Jessica Jones," Darrius said.

"Well she lied because her real name is Samantha Carr. She sometimes goes by the name Sam," Nelson said.

"Oh no, that's Lizeth's friend's name!" Darrius said.

"Man this girl is no friend to anyone. Lizeth may be in her way," Nelson said.

"I have to a call Lizeth. I am on my way home," Darrius said.

*****

Lizeth looked down at her phone, it was Darrius calling her again. She hit the ignore button. I don't feel like talking to him, right now is not the time, Lizeth thought to herself as she drove home in her company car. She was excited that she was able to clear up the issue at work. She planned to call the police once she got home. The commute was not that long from her job, so when she pulled up into her driveway she was a little more relieved. Darrius was still calling her phone non-stop. I hope nothing has happened, she thought. Lizeth got out of the car and made her way into the house. As she unloaded her things she was not aware of a dark figure walking up behind her.

Again her phone was ringing so she decided to answer. All she could hear Darrius say is, "Lizeth you're in danger!"

Someone snatched her phone from her ear and when Lizeth turned around she was face to face with the person pretending to be her. Lizeth was nervous and afraid, she did not know what to do. Here standing in front of her holding a gun, was someone dressed and looking identical to her, all the way down to her feet.

"Who are you?" Lizeth asked.

"I am Lizeth," the woman answered. Lizeth was even more shocked that this woman in front of her even sounded like her.

"Impressive isn't it?" the woman laughed.

"What is impressive?" Lizeth asked, even though she knew the answer.

"The fact that I look and sound just like you," she said.

"You're not me," Lizeth said.

"I am you, a better you," she said.

"You're fucking crazy," Lizeth said.

"Shut up and go into the study," she directed. Lizeth walked into the study where a chair was in the middle of the room, along with all the pictures of Darrius and all the many women he had been sleeping with.

"Sit in the chair!" she yelled. Lizeth could feel the cold hardness of the gun on her back as she pushed her towards the chair. Lizeth looked around the room for something to grab to get distance between her and this crazy woman.

She could see that the fire iron was standing up next to the chair. She also noticed that the room had plastic and sheets on the floor and walls. Lizeth had a bad feeling in her stomach that this woman came to kill her, as if she knew she would return home today. Lizeth reached for the fire iron and swung around, striking her in the hand and causing her to drop the gun. Lizeth struck her again, but this time it hit her in her face, causing the plaster on her face to rip, revealing her real identity.

Lizeth was paralyzed with disbelief, she could not move or speak. Staring at her was her friend of many years, Sam.

"Sam?" Lizeth said, baffled.

"My name is not Sam! It's Lizeth," she screamed. Sam grabbed the gun, ran up to Lizeth and struck her in her head, causing her to black out.

When Lizeth finally came to from having blacked out, she could not move her arms or her legs. Once her vision cleared up she could see that she was confined to the chair. Her head was throbbing really badly and she could see blood spots on her pants. Sam was pacing back and forth, talking to herself.

"She is not better than you, she is a loose end that must go," Sam said to herself, over and over. Sam began striking herself in the face. Lizeth began to get worried that she may not get out of this alive. Sam noticed that Lizeth was now awake.

"You bitch, this is your entire fault!" Sam screamed.

Lizeth was not sure what she was talking about, but she planned to keep her talking as much as possible.

"What did I do?" Lizeth asked, dazed.

"He is coming home to save you, and to think I planned on having you gone before then," Sam said.

"Why are you doing this?" Lizeth asked.

"Why do you think?" she said as she reached into her back pocket to retrieve the half-ripped photo of Darrius out of her pocket. "For him," she said as she kissed Darrius' face on the photo.

"You're crazy!" Lizeth said.

Sam laughed. "Yes I am, for him."

"He can't stand you, you delusional bitch!" Lizeth said.

Sam walked over to Lizeth and slapped her in her face.

"Bitch shut your mouth," Sam said. Lizeth could taste a bit of blood in her mouth. "Darrius has had me in more ways than one," Sam said with a devilish grin on her face.

She looked down to the photos on the floor of Darrius with all kinds of different women in provocative ways. Lizeth followed her eyes to all the photos on the floor. She had to admit that all of the photos were starting to make her feel some type of way. Sam could tell that she was uncomfortable. Sam laughed.

"You still don't get it!" Sam said. Sam began explaining it to her. She told her that she had been watching her every move since college. She tried then to break up the connection she and Darrius had but it was no use, he was in love with her. Then when they got married she told her it was no coincidence that they met, it was a set up since day one. "I had to keep you close to learn you," Sam said. Sam said that she intentionally lied to her so that she would end up leaving him, and when she did not leave him she had to take drastic matters. Sam picked up some of the photos from the floor and pushed them into Lizeth's face.

"You're so clueless," Sam said. "Look at the photos bitch, I am in all of them. I've had his dick in every hole in my body!" she screamed. "He has made me cum so many times. The way he sucks my breasts and puts his fingers in my pussy," Sam said with her eyes closed and her head tilted towards to the ceiling as if she was taking in a deep breath. "Woo! Just thinking about him is making me want to cum," Sam said, touching on herself.

Lizeth glanced down at the pictures and at first, she did not notice anything. All it looked like was a bunch of different women having sex with her husband. Then she noticed a mark on the backs of some of the woman in the photos. You would have to really look hard to see it, but it was there. Being that she was forced to look at the pictures, Lizeth felt that this woman was sick and maybe even more dangerous than she thought. Looking over these pictures, you would think it was all different women, only to find out that they all were the same person in each photo. Lizeth had to admit, she was well invested in what she was doing. She even fooled people at her job that she was her. Sam turned and lifted her shirt to show the mark on her back, the same mark that was on the backs of the women in the photos.

Chapter 10

Lizeth became angry and tried to get free. "You sick bitch!" Lizeth screamed.

Sam picked up a roll of tape and taped her mouth shut. She then went into the other room and when she came back, she had a pillow in her hand.

"Time for you to go," Sam said. Lizeth started to cry, she did not want to die like this. She had so many thoughts going through her head. She began to wonder where Darrius was. Even if he had left now from his parents' house he still would not get there in time. Why didn't I call the police before I got here? she thought. Lizeth was determined not to let it end like this. She started by trying to loosen the tape around her hands. Sam came and stood in front of Lizeth and placed the pillow in front of her head.

"No mess," Sam said. Lizeth could feel the tape loosening up. Sam pulled the trigger and the bullet hit Lizeth in her shoulder. Lizeth screamed in pain, but her adrenaline was just enough to help her break the hold of the tape from her hands. With all her strength, Lizeth charger forward and pushed Sam backwards. Her legs still tied to the chair and her shoulder bleeding, Lizeth tried to break free. Sam lost her hold on the gun. As it went across the floor to the opposite side of the room, she was on her back.

Sam flipped to her feet rather fast and grabbed Lizeth by her hair to pull her across the floor in the direction of the gun. Lizeth screamed in agony as she fought Sam's grip on her hair. Lizeth grabbed for Sam's legs, causing her to fall to the floor once again. Sam kicked Lizeth in her face and Lizeth fell back. As Sam went for the gun, Lizeth went to free her feet. Just as Sam reach the gun Lizeth got free and darted for the opposite room with Sam shooting after her. Lizeth ran toward the kitchen in search of a weapon, or phone.

Lizeth was starting to feel weak from the gunshot wound in her shoulder. She could hear Sam taunting her as she pulled the tape from her mouth off. Lizeth made it to the kitchen where she grabbed a knife. She then went to the phone and to her surprise still had a dial tone.

"Dumb bitch," Lizeth said. Lizeth ran from the kitchen as she could hear Sam getting close. She went through the kitchen to the dining room where she crouched beside her large china cabinet.

"Bitch where are you, why are you making this so hard?" Sam yelled as she stood in the kitchen.

"He doesn't want you, he wants me," Sam said as she started to cry. "He has told me so many times how much he loves me," Sam said. "Come out now," Sam screamed as she knocked some items off the counter down. Sam noticed that a knife and the cordless phone were missing. She rushed over and unplugged the phone.

"Didn't anyone ever tell you not to bring a knife to a gun fight? You bitch!" Sam shouted, getting angrier. The voices in her head started to talk to her again.

*****

Darrius called the police and told them that his wife was in danger. He tried calling the house, but Lizeth managed to call him before the phone line went out to let him know that Sam was there with a gun. A detective who was familiar with

Sam called him back to let him know that they were in route to his house. Darrius was nervous, the thought of losing Lizeth made him furious, because if anything happened to her it would be his fault.

Darrius managed to make it to the city rather quickly, but he was still a long ways out. He was hoping that the police would make it there in time. He was praying to God that Lizeth was still alive because she said she was hiding and she had a weapon. That's all he got to hear her say before the line went dead. Darrius prayed repeatedly in the car for the lord to keep her safe. "I can't lose her," Darrius said to himself.

*****

Lizeth could see that Sam was standing on the opposite side of the china cabinet.

"I know you're in here," Sam taunted. "The phone doesn't work," Sam shouted.

Lizeth remained and waited for her chance to catch her off guard. Sam started to walk alongside the china cabinet looking under the table, and once she turned to face the corner that Lizeth was in, Lizeth took the knife and stabbed her in her shoulder, causing her to drop the gun onto the ground. Sam screamed in pain.

"A shoulder for a shoulder bitch!" Lizeth said as she retrieved the gun. Sam pulled the knife out of her shoulder and charged at Lizeth. Lizeth turned and fired a warning shot in the air. Sam stopped in her tracks.

"Why won't you die?" Sam asked as she fell to her knees in tears.

Lizeth stood in front of Sam with the gun pointed at her. She realized at that moment that Sam was a very sick person who did not deserve to live. Lizeth didn't think she could take a life, however, she did not want to have to worry about this ever happening again.

"He is my husband," Lizeth said. Sam stopped her crying and started to laugh.

"Well he is your husband, and he is also my baby's father," Sam said with a devilish grin.

Lizeth could feel the anger boiling up inside of her. Was she telling the truth or was this a mind trick she was playing? How dare this crazy bitch have a child by my husband before me? Lizeth thought to herself.

"What, you're going to shoot a pregnant woman?" Sam

asked. Lizeth could hear the sounds of the sirens approaching her house in the distance.

"Yes, saved by the bell," Sam laughed.

"Shut up you psycho bitch," Lizeth said, still pointing the gun at Sam.

"You don't have it in you," Sam goaded.

Lizeth pulled the trigger and the bullet went past Sam's face. "I said shut up!" Lizeth shouted. Sam just stared at Lizeth with a smile on her face. The sirens were closer now. Sam spoke and said the few words that bothered Lizeth the worst.

"If they take me away, I will still have his child. He will not allow his child to go into a foster home," Sam said.

Lizeth knew this to be true. Darrius wanted a family and with everything going on, he definitely would not allow his child to be taken away from him. Lizeth had a choice to make. Spend the rest of her life alone or with the man she loved despite everything, along with a child he had with a crazy bitch.

"Decisions, decisions," Sam continued to taunt.

The police were now at the door, screaming for her to come out. Lizeth just stood there and for a moment, everything went in slow motion. She saw her life with

Darrius with this child, how she would always have the reminder of his infidelities. She saw them growing apart because she could not handle it. Lizeth didn't know when she closed her eyes, but when she opened them Sam was on her feet, standing directly in front of her about to stab her in her chest. Suddenly Lizeth heard a gunshot.

Lizeth watched as Sam fell to the ground, lifeless. The officers were screaming for her to drop the gun, but she was so stunned that she could not move. An officer came up alongside of her and whispered in her ear, "You're okay, you did not shoot her." Lizeth was sure she took her life. However, an officer had come from behind and shot Sam in the back, saving Lizeth's life.

Lizeth was escorted out of the house for the police to survey the house. She was taken to the hospital where they treated her for her gunshot wound and head wound.

Darrius looked on as Lizeth laid in the hospital bed recovering. She had lost a lot of blood so they kept her for observation. Today she would be able to go home with him and he was more than ready to take her home. Darrius had the house cleaned from top to bottom and a nice security system installed. Darrius even went out and bought a dog, as a gift for Lizeth. Lizeth opened her eyes and just stared at

Darrius, then looked around.

"How long was I out?" Lizeth asked.

"Three days," Darrius said. Lizeth tried to sit up only to see that her left arm was in a brace.

"The doctor said you had to wear that for a while," Darrius said as he noticed her looking at it.

"When do I get to leave?"

"They said later today if you're up for it."

"Ok." They just sat without saying much. A nurse came in and greeted them. She told Lizeth how happy she was to see that she was finally awake. She took her blood pressure and told her that she would let the Doctor know that she was awake now.

The doctor came in and checked Lizeth out. He told her that everything looked fine and she could go home today. The doctor also told her that she would need to make an appointment to see her gynecologist, because she was five weeks pregnant. A surprise for both Darrius and Lizeth.

The ride home was both bitter and sweet. Darrius told her about what he leaned about Sam, whose real name was Samantha. Nelson informed him and warned him about her. Lizeth told Darrius that all the women he was with were Sam. He told her that the detectives filled him in on everything. Sam was not pregnant and she was behind the stolen files from his job. As they pulled up to the house, Lizeth became filled with emotions and she broke down in tears.

"Lizeth are you okay?" Darrius asked.

"No I am not!" she cried.

"What can I do?" he asked.

"Don't put me through this again," she said.

"I promise you, I won't," he said with compassion.

"If you do I will leave you. Me and my child," Lizeth said.

Darrius jumped out of the car and ran to Lizeth's side to help her out of the car.

They walked inside to the living room and Lizeth could see that Darrius had done some redecorating. The house looked wonderful. There seemed to be new furniture and paintings. Lizeth loved that he fixed up the house, maybe making it easier for her to forget that horrible day.

"I hope you like what I did," Darrius said.

"I do, it's lovely," Lizeth said as she sat down on the big plush couch.

"I have another surprise for you," Darrius said.

Darrius walked out of the living room and came back

with a nice sized box in his hand. The box started to move. Lizeth got nervous, but the look in Darrius' eyes made her feel okay. She took the lid off and out popped the small head of a chocolate, Labrador puppy.

"He is so cute!" Lizeth said.

"I thought we needed a dog around here," Darrius said. Lizeth could see that he was trying. She gave him credit for trying, but she would never forget.

"What's his name?" Lizeth asked.

"I was waiting on you to name him," Darrius said. Lizeth thought about it for a minute.

"We can call him Jackson," she said.

Darrius smiled. "I like that."

*****

Six months later Lizeth was growing and the doctor had to put her on bed rest. However, the doctor did not know Lizeth very well, she was still getting around as if she was not pregnant. Darrius had to fuss with her to stay in the bed.

"Doctor's orders sweetheart," Darrius said as he kissed Lizeth on the forehead.

"That's not fair. I need to be there with you," Lizeth

protested.

"I will be fine," Darrius said.

"Fine, but are you sure?" Lizeth said.

"Yes," Darrius said.

Darrius enjoyed watching Lizeth get bigger with the growing life inside of her that they created together. Today was just one of those days she would have to miss. His father passed a few days ago. His sickness took an ugly turn for the worse and he died in his sleep. Darrius was glad that he made peace with his father before he left here. Today, Darrius was to meet his brother. His mother promised him that he and his twin brother would meet.

The service for his father was nice. His mother told him that his brother was running late and he would make it afterwards. Darrius thought she was bluffing. After the funeral service at the burial ground the family met up back at his mother's house. Darrius was standing next to his mother when he saw a familiar face in the crowd.

"Nelson, thank you for coming," Darrius said. Nelson just stood there looking confused.

"Likewise man," Nelson said. Darrius' mother walked up beside the two men.

"Hi boys, I see you have met each other," she smiled.

Both men looked at each other.

"I have known him for a while now," Darrius said. His mother looked to Darrius, and then to Nelson.

"Have you two really looked in a mirror? This is your twin brother," she said and walked off.

They just stood and looked at each other, both with mixed emotions, not knowing what to say to the other.

"How did I not see it?" Darrius asked.

"The same here," Nelson said.

Their mother took them into the kitchen with the same photo album she showed all the time and explained to them that if they looked at their childhood pictures, they both would see pictures that one didn't recall taking. Darrius was showed pictures of Nelson at a young age, and Nelson the same with Darrius. It all made sense to them now. Darrius' aunt adopted Nelson, so Nelson was not too far away. Both men were happy and pleased.

*****

Lizeth gave birth a few months later to a set of twin girls. She and Darrius were overjoyed with happiness. Lizeth took a less time consuming job and became a work at home mom. Darrius, wanting to help, allowed Nelson to handle his business for him while he stayed home with Lizeth to help raise the girls. Darrius moved his mother in and she sold the estate to his brother Travis. He and his ex-wife had gotten back together and he found out that the child she was carrying at one point was his. Things seemed to look up for the Jackson family, everything was going just great.

Lizeth went to answer the door as it seemed someone was knocking. Once she got to the door, she noticed a letter on the ground. When she opened the door, no one was there. She bent down to get the letter only to see that it was blank. She closed the door to find Sam standing directly behind her with a gun in her face.

"Not that easy bitch!" she said and pulled the trigger. Her body went into shock and she started to scream out.

"Noooo…Nooooo!" Lizeth screamed.

"Lizeth wake up babe, wake up," Darrius said. Lizeth opened her eyes to see Darrius lying next to her.

"Baby you were having a nightmare," he said.

"I was dreaming?" Lizeth said.

"Yes," Darrius nodded.

"But it felt so real. I saw Sam and she had a gun," Lizeth insisted.

"Sam is gone baby, she is not our problem anymore," Darrius said, kissing her on her forehead.

"You're right, it was just a dream," Lizeth said as she drifted back to sleep in Darrius' arms.

*****

Meanwhile at the hospital: A class of potential doctors and nurses were being escorted around the hospital learning about various patients.

"She has been in a coma for a long time now, we are not sure if she will ever come out," a male voice said.

"Sir, why are her hands chained up to the railing of the bed?" a female student asked.

"Good question. Well in this young lady's case, whose name we will not say due to HIPPA laws, she was considered a real threat to herself and others," he explained.

"Why a threat?" another student asked.

"Well she suffers from multiple personalities and anger issues. She is very cunning and is someone you would keep a close eye on. As you can see, there is an officer stationed at her door," he said. The entire class looked scared and interested at the same time.

"Well let's continue on our rounds," he said as he moved the class down the hall. However, not everyone left the room. A young woman stayed behind because she wanted to know the name of the mystery woman in the bed. Once everyone was out the room she went over to the bed and read her name on her wrist bracelet.

"Samantha Carr you don't look so scary," she said. She turned to leave the room but she heard a noise, and when she turned back around the bed was empty.

"Oh God!" Her legs became noodles. She was afraid. She turned to run out of the room but was stopped by an awakened Samantha Carr.

"Please don't hurt me," she pleaded. Sam did not say anything she just let the hospital door close.

"What is your name?" Sam asked.

"Gabby Williams," she answered.

"That's a nice name Gabby," Sam said with a devilish grin on her face.

"Are you going to kill me?" Gabby asked. Sam just looked at her as if she was taking photos of her face with her eyes. Gabby backed up and Sam walked towards her.

"I want your face," Sam said.

"What?" Gabby said, now more afraid.

"Yes, I think it will fit just fine," Sam said, pulling a scalpel from behind her back. Gabby tried to run but Sam quickly knocked her out.

Sam put Gabby in the shower in her room, tied her up, gagged her mouth and gave her a shot of anesthesia to keep her unconscious. When nightfall came and they did the routine bed check on her, she laid there as if she was still in the coma.

"She's fine, I think you can leave for the night officer. She has been sleep for six months, still no change," A nurse said to the officer posted outside her door.

"You're right, I will call my lieutenant," he agreed.

After the officer left and the nurse went back to her station, Sam got Gabby out of the shower and put her in a wheelchair. Sam looked out into the hall and it was clear. She knew the layout of the hospital because she had awakened from her coma three months earlier and each night she would go about the hospital unnoticed.

Sam took Gabby all the way down to the morgue where she had hidden some things prior to coming down here. She placed Gabby on to the metal table and began taking off her clothes. She went through her purse and took her cell phone as well. After she did that, she studied her body before she started to cut the skin from her face off.

Once it was off she put it in some solution to get it clean, and then matched it up to her own face until it lined up correctly. She applied the needed stuff to make sure it would not move and once complete, she looked into the mirror and was pleased with her work.

"Hi, I am Gabby Williams," Sam said, sounding exactly like Gabby. She changed into Gabby's clothes and picked up her purse. She turned on the furnace and threw her hospital gown and her bracelet in the fire. She hit the latch on the metal table that made Gabby slide into the furnace. Sam smiled and cleaned up her mess by burning any evidence. She walked up to the same floor she was on to test her work. Once she got around to the nurse's station, the nurse looked at her strangely.

"Hey you," the nurse said. Sam stopped as she had her scalpel ready. She turned to face the nurse.

"Yes?" Sam answered.

"Your class left hours ago, you have to sign out here," the nurse said.

"You're right, I do apologize." Sam signed her name Gabby Williams. She walked towards the door to freedom until the nurse called to her again.

"Hey Gabby," the nurse called out.

Sam's heart sunk in her chest. She thought for sure she was caught.

"Yes?" Sam answered.

"You might need to get your face looked at, it's bleeding," she said. Sam kept walking.

"Oh it's not my face," she said with a smile as she walked out of the hospital.

Made in the USA
Charleston, SC
10 February 2017